King of the Castle

by

SALLY WENTWORTH

Harlequin Books

TORONTO • LONDON • NEW YORK • AMSTERDAM • SYDNEY

Original hardcover edition published in 1978
by Mills & Boon Limited

ISBN 0-373-02185-2

Harlequin edition published August 1978

CHAPTER ONE

IT was one of the first really warm days of early June, full of the promise that only a spring day can bring. Already the city streets were beginning to fill as people emerged from their places of work to make the most of the lunch hour, either hurrying to restaurants or to do their shopping. As Lee Summers stepped through the swing doors of the modern, glass-fronted office block where she had worked as a secretary to a firm of solicitors for the last two years, she lifted her face gladly to the sun and shook her head to let the light breeze ruffle the mass of dark curls that framed her fine-boned face and long-lashed hazel eyes. It felt good to be out in the open again, away from the cluttered office with its aura of legal solemnity.

There was excitement in her step as she eagerly crossed the road and made her way along Fleet Street until she came to the lovely old arch that led into the Inns of Court. Once inside, the roar of the traffic was immediately cut off; there was an inner peace, a kind of oasis of quiet as she passed the ancient round walls of the twelfth-century Temple church. On either side of the tree-lined courtyard below her were the buildings of the Middle Temple stretching almost down to the river. Here the London barristers had their offices, where they could work in peace and quiet, but were conveniently situated close to the Law Courts in the Strand.

A familiar figure rose from a seat set under the frail

beauty of a silver birch tree and waved a hand in greeting. Lee waved back and ran down the steps towards him, her heels echoing on the old stone paving. She rushed into his outstretched arms and kissed him exuberantly.

'Hey, what have I done to deserve this?' There was surprise in Richard Derrington's voice as he looked at Lee in amusement.

'Oh, Richard, I've had the most wonderful news! I've inherited some property in Austria. Look, I'll show you.' Eagerly she pulled him back to the seat and took a letter from her handbag. 'The English isn't a hundred per cent perfect, but it's still quite easy to understand.'

Richard smiled indulgently as she thrust the letter under his nose but took his time as he examined the heading before going on to the contents.

'From the firm of Kreuz in Ausbach in the Tyrol district. Can't say I've ever heard of them before.'

'Never mind that, just read the letter,' Lee ordered impatiently. Then, restless with excitement, 'Oh, here, I'll read you the important bits. "Have to advise you of the death of your great-uncle, Herr Howard Canning ... He has left you his property known as the Chalet Alpenrose, which consists of a house and the surrounding land." Then he gives particulars of the land, but later on ... Oh, yes, here it is. "On the death of Herr Canning an offer was made for the property and I consider it to be a fair, if not generous, price, taking into account the fact that the house and land have been neglected during the last years of Herr Canning's ownership."' Her eyes shining, her face flushed with happiness, Lee added, 'Richard, you see what this means? We won't have to wait until you're established. We can get engaged this year—straight away!'

'Hey, hold your horses!' He laughingly took the

letter back from her and proceeded to read it thoroughly while Lee sat beside him with as much patience as she could muster.

She had first met Richard soon after starting work in the solicitors' office. As a very junior barrister, only recently called to the bar, he had come there on business and they had become on friendly terms. Gradually their relationship had developed into closeness and it was tacitly understood that they would marry when Richard had become more established in his profession. Lee would have been willing to take a chance and start married life now in a bedsit or a small flat, but Richard wouldn't hear of it and insisted that they wait until they could afford a decent house. He was a rather cautious person, but was kind and gentle; thoroughly nice, thoroughly reliable; a perfect foil for Lee's vital and impulsive nature. Often he had warned her against acting unwisely as she had plunged enthusiastically into some new scheme or hobby. She had been grateful for the warning, but sometimes, at the back of her mind, there were the slightest shades of regret for the lost opportunities, the experiences he had guided her away from.

'Who was this Howard Canning?' he asked. 'I've never heard you speak of him before.'

'I'd almost forgotten he existed,' Lee admitted. 'He was my mother's uncle and I used to see him quite often as a child, but then he married an Austrian woman and settled over there. Apart from an occasional Christmas card we haven't heard from him since. But I seem to remember Mother saying that he always had a soft spot for me.'

'Hm,' Richard looked up from the letter at last. 'It certainly seems very interesting.'

'Interesting! Is that all you can say? It's the most fantastic news I've had in years. Look, I worked out the offer this person has made for the land. In English money it comes to almost twenty-five thousand pounds. That's more than enough for a house. Oh, Richard, isn't it wonderful?'

He smiled down at her, pleased at her happiness and excitement, but said warningly, 'You just can't accept this offer, you know. You should really have an independent valuation of the land made before you agree on any price. It would be better if we could go over there and see it for ourselves; make sure it isn't planted with valuable crops or timber, or situated on the edge of a town, or an area that's about to be developed or something. But unfortunately I have that important case I told you about coming along shortly and I can't possibly get away before that; there's too much work to do on it.'

'But you said that the case could go on for weeks, even months.'

'Yes, I know. I'm sorry, but you know that it could lead to me getting some cases of my own and I can't possibly throw it up. But we'll go to Austria just as soon as it's finished,' he consoled Lee. 'Come on, we'd better go and eat before everywhere fills up.'

He began to walk her back towards the main road, but they had gone only a few yards before Lee caught his sleeve eagerly and pulled him round to face her.

'You can't go, but what's to stop me going by myself? I've got three weeks' holiday due to me and I could leave almost straightaway.'

Richard looked somewhat taken aback. 'But you can't go over there alone!'

'Why not? I'm twenty-one, and it's not as if I'm going to darkest Africa or something.'

'But you wouldn't know what to look for, wouldn't know if you were being cheated.'

'Then all I have to do is pick up the phone and ask

you for advice. Richard, don't be an old stick-in-the-mud. The prospective buyer might drop out if he's kept waiting indefinitely for an answer,' she pointed out.

'If he's interested then others might be as well.' Richard shook his head. 'I don't like to think of you going off and trying to handle things by yourself.'

Lee saw that it wasn't going to be easy and it took her all through their walk to a restaurant, and the whole meal right through to the coffee stage to wheedle, cajole and coax him into finally grudgingly agreeing.

'All right, but you've got to promise to get in touch with me if you have the slightest doubts, and you've definitely not to sign anything until you have sent me a photocopy—especially if it's in a language you don't understand.'

'Yes, I promise. You'll be my absentee legal adviser,' she placated him.

'I still don't like it,' Richard said worriedly. They walked back along Fleet Street and paused before the entrance to her office. He looked down at her severely. 'You've twisted me round your little finger again, haven't you?'

Lee grinned impishly up at him and then reached up to kiss him on the cheek. 'Yes,' she said softly, 'but look what it might lead to.' Then she laughed and waved as she turned to run into the building as the bells of the city churches chimed two o'clock.

In less than a week Lee had left the closely packed city streets behind and had flown to Munich, there to collect the little Volkswagen convertible that Richard had arranged to have waiting for her. Once having agreed, however reluctantly, to her going, he had been as thorough in helping her to make arrangements for the journey as he was in everything he did. She had written off to the firm of Austrian solicitors to let them know she was coming and had a long list of 'points to watch out for' that Richard had drawn up for her. He had checked to make sure she had everything and had still been uttering words of caution even after he had kissed her goodbye at the airport.

Lee smiled at him rather ruefully; he was a dear and she loved him, but he did tend to fuss over her, so that now it was almost a relief to be alone and to be driving along—very carefully because it was the first time she had ever driven on the wrong side of the road—between rolling fields and meadows with the distant massive greyness of the Alps coming ever nearer. Soon the road began to climb the foothills and the traffic thickened as cars and coachloads of tourists all headed for the mountain resorts and slowed down progress. At one o'clock Lee pulled off the switchback Alpine road and into the car-park of a restaurant built on the side of a mountain. She had been travelling for over three hours and needed a break. Securely locking the little yellow 'Beetle' as the hire agent had called it, Lee took her route map with her and found an empty table on the restaurant terrace, which had a terrific view and where she had the unnerving experience when looking out over the balcony of glancing down and seeing a four-thousand-foot drop below her. The terrace jutted out from the side of the mountain with nothing beneath it!

A smiling waitress dressed in the traditional dirndl skirt and embroidered blouse came to take her order, and Lee decided that as she was now in Austria she must try a wienerschnitzel. While she waited for her meal she studied the map and found that Ausbach seemed to be a smallish village set some distance away from the main tourist areas. She reckoned that she still had an hour's driving before she reached it; an hour of travelling along the winding road between these magnificent mountains which had an aged and mysterious atmosphere that she found difficult to define. But she didn't find them cold or overpowering; she loved the hills and climbing and felt perfectly at home here.

The waitress brought her lunch and after Lee had eaten the deliciously cooked veal cutlet she was again ready to cope with the unfamiliar roads and the erratic continental drivers. Ausbach proved to be situated some miles from the main highway and was reached by a fairly narrow road that twisted among the foothills of a range of smaller mountains, a road that crossed arched stone bridges over tumbling streams, passed fields of growing corn turning golden in the sun, and meadows reaching high into the hills where grazed herds of cows, the large bells strapped round their thick necks sounding a continuous peal that echoed back from the surrounding mountains. A dozen times Lee could have stopped to drink in the sights and sounds that were so new to her, but she was filled with a strange sense of unrest, a feeling that she must get to her destination before she gave herself the pleasure of revelling in this wonderful scenery.

When she finally arrived in Ausbach she found that the village was even more picturesque than she had imagined it could be. An onion-domed church dominated the village and the houses were of the wooden chalet type, with every available sill and ledge filled with window-boxes and hanging baskets gay with brightly coloured flowers. Lee stopped the car to exclaim with pleasure at the sight of the horse-trough and a large, hand-operated water pump beside it, all almost hidden under masses of blooms, but a harsh toot of a klaxon from a delivery van behind her reminded her that she was blocking the way. Realising that she had no idea where to find the solicitor's office, she pulled into a garage on one side of the village square to ask directions.

A mechanic in grubby overalls with a grizzled moustache looked up from under the bonnet of a large grey Mercedes at the far side of the forecourt. Wiping his greasy hands on a rag, he came over to her. '*Guten Tag, Fräulein. Bitte?*'

'Good afternoon. I wonder if you can help me? I'm trying to find the office of Herr Kreuz. Can you tell me how to get there, please?'

The man shrugged, '*Ich verstehe Sie nicht,*' and shook his head to show that he didn't understand.

Lee tried again more slowly. 'Herr Kreuz in the Brunnerstrasse. How do I get there?'

This time she had better luck, for he repeated the name after her, although it didn't sound quite the same as Lee had pronounced it. She rather wished that she had taken that course in German at school, but unfortunately she had chosen business studies instead. Now the man was pointing, but not as Lee had expected in the direction of one of the roads leading from the square, but to the doorway of the garage office which a man was just leaving. She looked at the attendant in some bewilderment, thinking that he must have misunderstood her after all, but he was very insistent, pointing again at the man and pushing her slightly towards him.

Rather hesitantly she approached the stranger, who was smartly but conservatively dressed and looked to be in his early thirties, but her main impression was that he certainly belonged here, for he was so tall that he towered over her just as the mountains towered over the village. 'Er . . .' Lee began, and then stopped.

'*Fräulein?*' The voice was extremely polite, but there was a look of amusement in the man's intensely blue eyes as he noticed her discomfiture.

'Excuse me, but do you speak English?'

'Sufficiently to help you, *Fräulein*, if you're in any difficulty,' he replied fluently and with hardly a trace of the guttural accent Lee had noticed in the other English-speaking Germans and Austrians she had encountered.

'Oh, good. That must be why the attendant pointed you out to me,' she said with some relief. 'You see, I asked him the way to Herr Kreuz's office in the Brunnerstrasse, but he doesn't speak English.'

But the man was hardly listening to the end of her explanation. A look of surprise had come into his eyes at the mention of Herr Kreuz and he was looking at her more closely.

'You are not a tourist, *Fräulein*?' The question was asked very casually, but the stranger was studying her now with some interest.

'Why, no, I have some business in Ausbach. Do you know the way, please?'

'Yes, the office isn't far from here. You turn left out of the garage and then take the second turning on the right, where the corner house has a double balcony and flower paintings on the walls; you can't mistake it. Herr Kreuz's office is halfway along the road.'

'Thank you, that's very kind of you.'

'Not at all, *Fräulein*. It is my pleasure.'

He bowed formally and Lee found herself flushing slightly as she looked up into blue eyes that regarded her intently and continued to watch her until she had climbed back into the car and driven away.

After that the way was easy to find, and she smiled as she passed the house on the corner; in England the landmark would have been a public house or a church, but here it was a house, not only with the usual window-boxes full of blooms, but also with Alpine flowers painted on every space of wall. Herr Kreuz's 'office' turned out to be a small wooden house with a low-eaved roof that jutted over the road and cast a shadow over the doorway as Lee rang the bell. A cat rose from a patch of sun and stretched lazily before stepping daintily over to inspect her, its amber coat rippling in the sunlight.

'Hallo, cat, do you speak English?' Lee murmured as she bent to stroke him. The cat purred and rubbed himself against her legs. He was evidently an all-language cat.

The door opened above her and Lee stood up to confront the small, neat woman who faced her.

'Good afternoon. Please, do you speak English?' Lee was rapidly coming to realise that this must be the opening gambit in any conversation.

The woman smiled. 'I speak a little. Are you Fräulein Summers?'

Lee gave a little sigh of relief. 'Yes, I am. You had my letter?'

'Oh, yes. Please, come in.' The woman stepped aside and motioned Lee into a pleasant, cool room that was more like a living-room than an office. 'Please to sit down.'

Lee did so and the cat immediately jumped on her lap and nudged her arm until she started stroking him again. 'Is Herr Kreuz in?'

'No, I am sorry. I am his secretary and I ...' she hesitated for the word, 'I keep house for him. I would have written to you, but there was no time, you come too soon behind your letter.'

It took Lee a moment to understand this, but then she said, 'But why should you wish to write to me when you knew I was coming?'

'It is because Herr Kreuz had to go to Vienna yesterday. Most important. He will not be back for two or three days.'

Lee looked at the woman in dismay. 'But is there no one else? Hasn't he a partner?'

'No, there is just Herr Kreuz. If you give me the telephone number of your hotel, I will let you know when he comes back.'

'I haven't booked into a hotel yet,' Lee told her. 'I came straight here. Perhaps you could recommend one?'

'The Hotel Erlenbach is good. It is near the main square.'

Lee thanked the secretary and drove slowly back the way she had come, feeling very disappointed at the news that Herr Kreuz would be away for another three days. She sighed with vexation. Richard wouldn't actually say 'I told you so' when she rang him tonight, but he would certainly think it. Going past the garage where she had stopped for directions, she looked to see if the tall stranger was still there, but both he and the large grey Mercedes had gone. She wondered if the car belonged to him, and somehow thought it did; both the size and the expensive sophistication of the vehicle seemed to suit him admirably.

The Hotel Erlenbach was situated just off the main square, a solid old building with carved wooden balconies and a large oak door that stood invitingly open. As it was still early in the season there was no difficulty in booking a room and a smiling hotelier showed her to a balconied room in the rear of the building with a large, high bed and rich wooden furniture. After unpacking her suitcase and changing into a dress, Lee joined the small group of guests who were making their way down to dinner. This was served in a quaint, beamed dining-room where she sat alone at a small table by a window that looked out over the valley towards the distant snow-capped peaks of the Alps.

Her fellow guests seemed to be a mixture of people passing through, commercial travellers, and a few hardy types on walking holidays. As none of them appeared to be English, Lee had only her beautifully cooked meal to concentrate on and had soon finished. There was little point in lingering, so she went out to make her telephone call to Richard; he should have left the Law Courts by now and be at home in the flat he shared with two other junior barristers. Herr Gruber, the proprietor, contacted the operator for her, but Lee was disappointed to find that there was a delay in placing calls to London.

'Perhaps, *Fräulein*, you would care to wait in the bar?' the hotelier suggested. 'There are magazines in English for you to look at and I will be sure to let you know as soon as your call comes through.'

There were already several people in the bar when Lee went in, mostly hotel guests, but also a few groups of villagers enjoying a social evening. Over in one corner an old man played an accordion, not loudly, but as a pleasant background to the talk and laughter. Finding herself an empty table in a quiet corner, Lee ordered a drink from the young waiter and looked around her. Against one wall was a huge, now empty, fireplace that she was sure must give out a roasting heat in the winter when the hotel was full of skiers, and decorating the old dark-panelled walls there were innumerable cow-bells suspended on thick leather straps patterned with brass studs. The atmosphere was warm and friendly, and Lee was glad that she had decided to wait here instead of in her room.

The English magazines were mostly tourist brochures with some wonderful photographs of the Tyrol, and Lee thoroughly enjoyed looking at them, determining to spend a proper holiday here and really see all the sights some indeterminate time in the future. Seeing all the maps on a nearby shelf, she realised that Ausbach must be a centre for walkers and hikers who were content to explore the foothills of the smaller mountain slopes rather than climb the higher peaks. The brochures exhausted, she casually took one of the maps and found it to be a large-scale plan of the district. One of the advantages of a map was that it could be understood no matter what language it was printed in, and Lee had soon picked out the village and was searching diligently to see if she could find the chalet her great-uncle had left her. As she had no idea in which direction it was situated it took her some time and she had almost come to the conclusion that it was too small to be marked, when she finally came upon it.

The Chalet Alpenrose. It was hardly any wonder that it had been difficult to find, for it was about three miles from the village itself and there was no road within half a mile of it, only the dotted line of a track or path leading towards it and then veering off for another half mile or so before crossing the closely drawn rows of lines that denoted a steep rise in ground to the outline of a large building marked as 'Schloss Reistoven'

Schloss, Lee mused; that must mean castle. Once or twice on her journey here she had glimpsed the far turrets of an ancient castle set atop lofty crags of rock, and from the markings on the map this Schloss Reistoven appeared to be the same. She wondered if the castle was a ruin or whether it was still in one piece, and, if so, whether it was open to tourists. It would be interesting to see a medieval fortress and would help to pass the time before Herr Kreuz returned from Vienna. But now her eyes returned eagerly to the little dot that was the Chalet Alpenrose. She smiled to herself; to think that she actually owned that little black square—it was still almost unbelievable! If only the road had gone anywhere near it she could have gone to see it by herself tomorrow, although she supposed that the solicitor would have the key and she wouldn't be able to see the inside. But there must be some way to reach it even if she parked the car and walked. Carefully she studied the terrain, noting that the chalet was sited on a piece of rising ground overlooking a valley guarded by trees. But of course, if she could hire a horse she could reach the chalet easily and have a pleasant ride through the countryside. Why hadn't she thought of that before?

So intently was she studying the map that Herr Gruber had to call her name twice before she realised that her call to Richard was through.

'Lee, are you all right? No accidents on the way?'

'No, of course not. I drove very carefully.'

'What did the solicitor have to say?'

Lee decided that a little prevarication would do no harm. 'We're not going to discuss anything until I've seen the chalet. I'm going to have a look at it tomorrow,' she added, being now fully determined to do just that.

'Well, don't forget what I told you. Don't let yourself be pushed into doing anything in a hurry.'

'No, I won't,' Lee assured him a trifle impatiently. 'I'll call you again when I have some news.'

'All right. Take care of yourself, darling.'

'And you. 'Bye!'

Still clutching the map, Lee made her way to her room intending to study it further, but once there she pushed open the door on to the balcony to look out at the night and then caught her breath in wonder. The map forgotten, she sat on a chair, leaned her elbows on the carved balcony and let the next hour slip away as she watched the snow on the high peaks gradually colour and then turn a bright, fluorescent pink as the sun slowly set behind the mountains.

The clamour of cow-bells woke her early the next morning, the unusual sound bringing her wide awake as the noise and roar of traffic would never have done. Pulling on a wrap, Lee pushed open the wooden doors on to the balcony and leaned out to gaze her fill at the bright spring morning. Although it was barely six o'clock the sun was already quite warm and was licking the dew from the grass and hedges. The air was filled with the rich scents of flowers that filled the boxes on her balcony; bees hummed in and out of nodding Canterbury bells, their buzzing lost in the sound of the cow-bells as the herds meandered their way back up the hill sides after the morning milking.

Lee felt an irresistible urge to be out in the open, breathing the good clean air and feeling the sun warm upon her back. Quickly she showered in the tiny bathroom opening off her room and changed into a clean shirt and comfortable faded jeans, then ran downstairs to breakfast, impatient not to lose a minute of this lovely day. She was one of the first guests down and soon finished the still warm croissants spread with home-made butter and jam and the little jug of coffee.

Herr Gruber was looking through the morning papers when she sought him out at the reception desk.

'Good morning.' She greeted him with the smile that lit her face.

Although rather a taciturn man, he smiled in return at her youth and vitality. '*Guten Morgen, Fräulein* Can I help you?'

'Yes, please. Is there anywhere around here where I can hire a horse?'

Herr Gruber's eyebrows rose at this unexpected request and he pulled at his full, flowing Franz Josef moustache in some perplexity. 'Well now, let me think.

There are no stables where you can hire an animal, *Fräulein*, but I have an old friend, Hans Schneider, who has a farm outside the village and who has a riding horse. He may be prepared to let you borrow the animal if he does not require it.'

'Is he on the phone? Could you ask him for me?' Lee asked eagerly.

'I will try, *Fräulein*.' He dialled the number and held quite a long conversation with his friend before putting down the receiver and nodding at Lee. '*Ja*, Fräulein Summers, Hans says he does not need the horse today and will be happy to lend it to you, if you are sure you can manage it. It is a—how do you say it —a young, fiery horse. Do you understand?'

'Yes, I understand. I'll go and take a look at him. Would you fix me up a sandwich lunch to take with me, please?'

Lee ran upstairs to change her sandals for more suitable shoes and then collected her packed lunch from the proprietor. He had drawn her a little sketch showing the way to the farm and she also took along the map she had found in the bar.

Hans Schneider was waiting for her in his stable-yard and a boy brought out the horse for her to see. It was a young chestnut with flowing mane and tail and a long white blaze down his head. Gently but confidently, Lee went up to him and began talking to him softly before stroking his neck. He pranced and snorted a little, but when she pulled some sugar lumps stolen from the hotel dining-room from her pocket, he deigned to overcome his haughtiness and lowered his proud head to eat from her hand.

The farmer nodded and smiled. '*Jawohl*, is good,' he said, and added instructions to the boy in German to saddle the chestnut.

Soon Lee was riding the horse easily along the edge

of the pine woods on the lower slopes of the hills, her lunch and the map safely stowed away in a bag hung from the saddle. Having been brought up in the country she had learnt to ride from an early age and felt perfectly at home in the saddle, although she had had little practice since she had been going out with Richard. As he did not ride himself, Lee had felt obliged to accompany him on rounds of golf or play tennis with him whenever they had spent a weekend or holiday at her home.

When the onion-shaped dome of the village church came in sight she paused to take out the map and to trace her route up into the mountains. Ausbach was soon found, and, having a good geographical memory, Lee was able to pick out the way that she would need to take to bypass the village and reach the chalet. The route would take her through the forest and above the castle and from there north-eastwards along the track that led to the chalet. Carefully she memorised the way she must take, then put the map away and urged the horse towards the forest and distant mountain peaks.

As the morning passed the glistening sunshine became more intense and she was glad to ride under the shade of the evergreen trees. The horse picked his way surely through the undergrowth, the fallen twigs and small branches making sharp cracking sounds as the weight of horse and rider snapped them in two. The ground began to rise more steeply now so that once or twice Lee dismounted to lead the horse up the steeper parts, and several times they forded icy streams. Rabbits and one or two deer scuttled away at their approach, but of other humans there was no sign; she was alone and content to be so.

At last they were above the vastness of the forest out on to the mountainside where the trees were less thick, and here Lee paused to take in her giant's view of the valley below. Ausbach looked like a toy village from here, like a collection of doll's houses waiting for little girls to come and play with them.

'Come on, boy, we should be there soon.' The horse pricked up his ears and started off again. After a further twenty minutes of steady climbing Lee gave a gasp of surprised pleasure, for there, in a clearing, was a small hut almost hidden among the trees. It was solidly built of logs and sheltered on two sides by an angle in the side of the mountain. Lee slipped from the saddle and tied the horse to a nearby tree before going to take a closer look. There were stacks of newly chopped wood on one side of the sturdy door and for a moment she wondered uneasily if anyone lived there. Well, there was only one way to find out.

She stepped up to the door and knocked as loudly as she could. She waited breathlessly, but the only sound was that of the horse gently cropping the grass. Slowly she put up her hand and lifted the latch, feeling rather ridiculously like Little Red Riding Hood. But there was no wolf awaiting her, only an empty hut furnished rather sparsely with two bunk beds on the side nearest the mountain, a table and two chairs and a small cupboard near a big, pot-bellied stove. It must have provided a welcome haven to anyone lost or stranded on the mountain in winter, but on this sunny day it was less than inviting and Lee soon came out into the open again. Nearby a stream had been partially dammed to create a small pool, and she took advantage of it to water the horse before unsaddling him and sitting down beside it to eat her lunch.

The ride had given her an appetite, so she opened her lunch bag to find crispy rolls, hard-boiled eggs and fruit. She began to eat hungrily and it was several minutes before the flashes of light caught her eye. They didn't come from the village, but from a building about

a mile further east; a building whose towers and battle-
ments soared gracefully into the sky, a fairytale castle
set like a jewel in this lovely countryside. This must be
the Schloss Reistoven she had seen marked on the map,
she realised. The brief flash of light came again, as if
the sun was reflecting on some bright moving object;
not a window because it wasn't big enough, and there
appeared to be two reflections close together. They
seemed to be coming from a room in one of the towers.

Hastily Lee scrambled to her feet, her lunch forgotten, and ran to her saddlebag where she took out the
small but powerful pair of binoculars that she had
brought with her in case she saw an unusual bird or
animal. Running back to the pool, she quickly focussed
them on the turret where she had seen the flashes. Yes,
she was right! Someone was watching her through
their own binoculars. For a moment the twin points of
light were perfectly still as if whoever it was had been
taken aback to see her returning the scrutiny, then
they disappeared. Lee saw a brief movement behind the
window, but could make out no details of her observer.

For several minutes she continued to watch the
tower, but there was no further sign of life and eventually she sat down by the stream again and finished her
lunch. The scent of alpine flowers hung heavy on the
air, butterflies flickered at the water's edge and birds
called to one another as they busily fed their young.
Lee leant back on the bank and felt the sun warming
her like a blanket. Before long she was fast asleep, like a
modern Titania, alone but for the animals and birds
around her.

Perhaps it was some primeval awareness of danger,
perhaps only a shadow blocking out the sun that
brought her suddenly and rudely awake. She opened
her eyes and saw a man standing over her! Instantly
she sat up, pieces of grass still clinging to her dark

curls. Then, with an intense feeling of relief, she recognised the man she had met at the garage yesterday, the man who had directed her to the solicitor's house.

He towered over her, his expression unreadable as he looked down at her. 'Ah, the young English lady.' Then, seeing her eyes still wide with alarm, he added, 'I'm sorry, I didn't mean to startle you,' and reached down to help her to scramble to her feet.

'It's—it's all right, really. It was just being woken up so suddenly.' The shock had left Lee feeling strangely breathless and she could hear her heart beating in her chest.

The big man smiled slightly as he said, 'I came to order off a trespasser and I find instead a Sleeping Beauty.'

'A trespasser? Is this land private, then?'

'I'm afraid so, *Fräulein*. You are well over half a mile on to the Von Reistoven estates.'

Flushing slightly, Lee said, 'I'm sorry, I had no idea. There weren't any fences or hedges and it didn't say anything on the map—or at least I didn't think it did.'

'You intended to come this way? You're not lost?'

'Oh, no, I was making my way across to the other side of the castle, but I found the hut and the stream and it all looked so—so enchanting that I just had to stop,' she explained. 'But how did you know I was here? I didn't . . .' Then she broke off, remembering how someone had watched her from the castle turret.

As if reading her thoughts the stranger said, 'You must forgive me, *Fräulein*, but often we get tourists wandering through the woods who do a great deal of harm to the environment, so we try to discourage them as much as possible.' He paused. 'But you said that you were on your way somewhere?'

'Yes, to the Chalet Alpenrose. I'll be getting along now.'

Lee went to turn away, but he raised a hand to detain her. 'Then I was right in my surmise yesterday; you are the niece of Herr Canning?'

Eyebrows raised in surprise, Lee answered, 'His great-niece, yes. But how did you know?'

'I knew that Herr Canning had left his—er—property to a young English girl and I knew that Herr Kreuz was his solicitor, so when you asked me the way to his office I put two and two together and ...'

'And came up with the right answer,' Lee finished for him. 'Did you know my great-uncle well, Herr ...?'

'Your pardon, *Fräulein*.' Slowly, his eyes on her face, he said, 'Max von Reistoven.' As he introduced himself he gave her a small bow that somehow didn't seem at all incongruous when he did it.

'Von Reistoven? But isn't that the name of the castle I saw marked on the map?'

'The Schloss Reistoven, yes. You can see it quite clearly from here—especially if you look through binoculars,' he added wryly.

Lee glanced quickly up at him, but saw only amusement in his eyes. 'It was your own fault, you started watching me first,' she retorted with a smile, and then turned to look again at the fairytale castle. 'Do you really live there?'

'Why, yes.'

Lee swung round to stare at him. 'You don't—you don't own that lovely place?'

He smiled rather enigmatically. 'It belongs to my family. But you said that you were on your way to your own inheritance. What did you think of it?' he asked carefully, his eyes again on her face.

'I haven't seen it yet. Herr Kreuz is away in Vienna and not expected back for a couple of days. That's why I'm going there now. I haven't got the keys, of course, but at least I'll be able to look at the chalet from the outside.'

'So you haven't yet seen Herr Kreuz,' Max von Reistoven said, almost to himself. Then, rather as if he had made up his mind about something, he added, 'May I then be permitted to guide you the rest of the way? It's easy enough to find, but I wouldn't want you to fall in with any of our foresters—they have orders to turn any tourists away.'

'That's very kind of you, Herr von Reistoven, but I wouldn't want to take you out of your way.' Lee felt rather disconcerted by his offer and wasn't sure whether she wanted to accept it or not.

'It is no trouble, *Fräulein*. Let me saddle your horse for you.'

Lee began to protest half-heartedly, but he had already lifted the heavy saddle and thrown it easily across the horse's back. While he concentrated on his task Lee was able to take a closer look at him. She supposed that he wasn't exactly handsome; his face was too strong for that, with a very firm chin that looked used to having its own way, a rather rugged profile and a high forehead partly obscured by a sweep of thick fair hair. He turned and met her gaze, a slight quirk on his lips as he saw that she had been studying him.

'But you haven't yet told me your name, *Fräulein*,' he reminded her.

'It's Summers. Lee Summers.'

He nodded and turned back to the horse. 'This is a good animal.' After buckling the saddle strap, he ran his hands lightly over the animal, expertly assessing him, and the chestnut stayed still beneath the inspection as he felt the strength and mastery of those hands. 'I'm sure I've seen him before. Doesn't he belong to Herr Schneider?'

'Yes, he does.'

'He's a strong young horse. Are you sure you can handle him?'

Lee turned to him with some annoyance in her eyes. 'Yes, Herr von Reistoven, I'm quite sure I can handle him,' she said tartly.

One eyebrow was raised quizzically as he smiled with genuine amusement before raising his hands in mock fright. 'I humbly beg your pardon, *Fräulein*, I stand corrected.'

Lee laughed at his expression and let him give her a leg up. His own horse was tethered nearby; a magnificent black beast that quite dwarfed Lee's chestnut and made her feel as if she was riding a pony. 'That's quite an animal you have there,' she remarked, then added with studied innocence, 'Are you sure you can handle him, Herr von Reistoven?'

Despite his size, Max von Reistoven vaulted lightly into the saddle and then turned to look at her. 'So you've claws, have you?' He bent to take hold of her bridle to lead her along.

Lee drew back on the reins and said very clearly, 'Please take your hand from my bridle.'

He looked frowningly at her for a moment, but she stared back at him defiantly. 'Ah, yes,' he said softly. 'I'd forgotten you were English,' and let go of the bridle.

Looking at him suspiciously, Lee said, 'What does that mean?'

As he urged his horse along the path, he answered, 'It means that most of the English people I've known are exceedingly stubborn, and it would appear that the members of your family are exceptionally so.'

Lee smiled. 'You must have known my great-uncle well if you knew that. Were you his friend?'

He was riding ahead of her, so she couldn't see his expression as he replied slowly, 'No, I wasn't a friend,

but I knew him well enough to say that he was the
most obstinate man I have ever met!'

During the ride he politely pointed out different
flowers and plants for her attention, his knowledge of
the forest seemingly endless. 'The hills are usually safe
enough in summer, but sometimes we get bears that
wander across the Bavarian border from the National
Park.'

'Are they dangerous?' Lee enquired.

'They can be nasty if they're hungry, but usually
they're more frightened of you than you are of them.'

Lee laughed, her face alight with amusement, 'Somehow I wouldn't like to take a bet on that!'

He smiled at her again and went on to talk about
other things, but Lee couldn't help noticing the way his
eyes crinkled up at the corners, making his features so
different from his usual rather stern and autocratic
look.

That look was back on his face now as they reached
a nursery of young pines covering several acres, the
trees carefully planted in spaced straight lines, the
ground between them kept clear of scrub and undergrowth.

'This is part of the re-afforestation programme.' he
told her. 'For every tree we cut down for timber, another is planted and will eventually grow to take its
place. A continuous cycle, you see, unless,' he added
rather grimly, 'the trees are attacked by diseases and
blights from old decaying trees and vegetation. Such as
that.'

He had come to a halt and pointed with his riding
crop across a wide firebreak to a thickly wooded stretch
of land where the trees and bushes were densely packed
together, fighting for light and air, the tree trunks almost smothered with ivy, creeper and other clinging
parasites.

As she remembered how beautifully kept and tended the forest they had ridden through had been, Lee looked at him in astonishment.

'But why don't you clear it, then?'

Max von Reistoven turned to look at her, an enigmatic expression on his features. 'Because, Fräulein Summers, it isn't mine to clear. We have reached the boundary of the Von Reistoven estates, and that piece of land is the beginning of your inheritance!'

CHAPTER TWO

RATHER numbly, Lee turned back to look at the choked woodland. To say anything seemed rather inadequate, so she merely urged the horse forward until they came to the firebreak.

'Is there a way through?' she asked.

'I seem to remember a path over to the left.' Max led the way to an overgrown track where they had to continually push branches out of the way and could make only slow progress. After about ten minutes Lee glimpsed sunlight ahead of them and they emerged into a meadow of waist-high grass which sloped down to a chalet house of dark wood set on a piece of level ground that looked out over a flower-banked stream and gently rolling pastures to the valley below.

Lee drew in a breath of pure delight. It was a scene lovely enough to grace a calendar; the sun shining across the peaceful valley, the sound of cow-bells echoing through the hills as the cattle moved placidly across the fields, the rich scent of flowers, but most of all the sun-lapped house set so cosily in the fold of the hill. Eagerly Lee heeled the horse towards it, her eyes drinking in each detail of the house; the outside stair-way leading to a carved balcony with a heavy door opening off it along the front of the first floor, the shuttered windows, and the roof that overhung the balcony to give protection from the weather. Max von Reistoven rode alongside her, observing her face lit up with pleasure and excitement at this first glimpse of her legacy.

As they drew nearer Lee could see the house more clearly and the horse slowed as she lowered the reins. The sun still shone on the windows, but now she could see that most of them were broken and the shutters hanging askew. Some of the logs that formed the roof had come loose and fallen to the ground leaving a gaping hole open to the weather, and the lovely carved balcony was warped and broken.

Lee brought the horse to a halt. 'Why didn't you tell me?' she asked in little more than a whisper, her eyes still taking in the poor, neglected house.

'I thought it better that you should see for yourself, *Fräulein*,' he told her, his voice gentle.

'It's almost derelict.'

'Yes, I'm afraid so. Would you like to see inside?'

'Can we get in?'

'It shouldn't be too difficult.' They dismounted and Max von Reistoven tied the horses to a post near an old horse-trough full of leaves and debris and with weeds growing from it.

'You'd better let me go first in case the stairs aren't safe,' he said.

'Why can't we get in through the ground floor?' Lee asked as she watched him cautiously testing each step before putting his weight on it.

'Because it was only used for housing the cattle during the winter time,' he explained.

'You mean the people lived over the cattle?' Lee asked in horror.

He grinned. 'It helped to keep the house warm. Many farmers still live that way, but I don't think your great-uncle ever used it for that purpose, only to store wood and provisions for the winter. Be careful of this step, it doesn't feel too sound.'

Gingerly Lee followed him up the staircase and on to the balcony. The heavy wooden door was firmly locked, but it took Max von Reistoven only a minute to put his arm through the broken window and reach down to open the latch. Pushing the window wide, he said, 'Would you like to go first, *Fräulein*?'

'Er—no, I think I'll let you lead the way,' Lee said after a quick look at the dark interior.

'Very wise.' He put a long leg over the sill and ducked inside. He took a look round and then came to help her to climb through the window. 'It's all right, there aren't any tramps or hikers camping out here.' He put his hands round Lee's slim waist and almost lifted her through.

'Oh!' She landed beside him rather breathlessly. 'I hadn't thought of that. Do you think anyone else has broken in?'

'I shouldn't be surprised. This looks as if it was a bedroom. Do you see that deep recess beside the fireplace? That was probably the box-bed where the children slept.'

Lee went over to look more closely. With its deep shelf of wooden planks the recess looked as if it would have made a far from comfortable bed, but she could see where the remains of a once-gay curtain hung from brass hooks.

'There would probably have been a big, carved bed in the room for the parents,' he told her. 'With perhaps a chair and a cupboard, and there would certainly have been a large oak chest where the wife would have kept all the linen that she brought with her as her dowry.'

Lee gazed round the room, imagining it as it must once have been; a carved and polished wooden bed with a white lace cover or perhaps a patchwork quilt, the room scrubbed clean and shining with colourful rugs on the floor and pretty curtains at the windows, and the scent of flowers instead of the damp, musty smell that hung uncleanly on the air. Max von Reistoven opened the door into another room that was obviously a kitchen-cum-living-room, for there was a huge iron range set into the stone chimney breast and a deep, cracked old sink in the corner. This room, too, was as neglected as the bedroom and Lee gave an involuntary shudder as a floating cobweb touched her face.

'I believe Herr Canning had part of the bedroom partitioned off to form a bathroom,' Max von Reistoven remarked. 'But of course, the water all had to be brought up by hand from the stream and then heated on the stove.'

Lee looked rather distastefully at the rusty old stove and the great patch of fungus and mildew that had formed on the wall. 'Do you mean my great-uncle actually lived here?'

'Ja, for some years until his wife died. But then, of course, they had a servant to look after them.' He opened a small door that Lee had thought was a cupboard. 'See, here's the stairway up into the attic where the servant would have lived. Would you like to go up there?'

'I suppose I'd better,' Lee said rather doubtfully as she looked behind the door and saw the narrow, unlit flight of steps.

He squeezed himself inside, his head crouched down to avoid the ceiling and his shoulders brushing the walls on either side even though he had turned sideways. Lee managed far more easily and found herself standing beside him in a low attic room lit only by a small dormer window and, of course, the light coming from the hole in the roof. The birds seemed to have made a haven of the place, for she could see several nests, both new and old, and the floor was white with bird droppings. An old broken bed stood against the wall near the chimney and the pipe from the stove went through the room, but otherwise there was no other heating for the poor servant who had spent his winters beneath the weight of snow pressing on the roof so close above his head.

Lee shivered despite the heat of the day. 'I think I've seen enough now, thank you.' She couldn't wait until they were out of the house and back in the sunlight again.

It was a relief to breathe the fresh, sweet air, to smell the flowers and to feel the sun warm on her face again. She sat down on the grass some way from the house but where she could still see it and Max von Reistoven dropped lightly down beside her. For a few moments she thought wistfully again of how the chalet must once have looked, then turned to find him watching her, a speculative look in his eyes.

'Please tell me what happened to the house. Why did Uncle Howard let it fall into such a state of decay?'

He chewed reflectively on a grass stalk before saying, 'Herr Canning was an old man, Fräulein Summers. He was also very obstinate. This house and the land was his wife's dowry, and she also had an annuity which paid for the servant and the upkeep of the land with enough left over to keep them in comfort. But when she died the annuity ceased. If your great-uncle had,' he hesitated, 'accepted the help and advice that was offered him, he could have worked the land and made a living from it, but, as I said, he was very stubborn and insisted on doing things his own way, and they didn't pay off. You can't run an Austrian mountain farm like you can an English downland one, and so he lost money. Soon he didn't have enough to pay the servant; then there was a landslide that blocked the stream for a while so that he didn't have any water.'

He threw down the straw rather angrily. 'Still the stubborn old fool—man,' he corrected himself hastily, 'wouldn't accept any help; blaming his neighbours for all that went wrong. In the end he had to leave here and went to live in Ausbach, but he refused to let anyone else tend the land with the result that, over the last few years, it has become the wilderness that you see, the trees overrun by parasites and disease and the undergrowth full of wild animals that get into my plantations and kill the young trees,' he finished vehemently.

'I—I see.' And Lee could see, more than he had told her. 'You're the person who has made the offer to buy the place, aren't you?'

A rather rueful look came over his face. 'Was it so obvious? I'm sorry, I hadn't meant to ... *Ja*, I admit this piece of land has been a thorn in my flesh for some years, and when I heard that Herr Canning had willed it to you, well ...' He shrugged, a typically continental gesture. 'It seemed like an ideal opportunity to buy the land and clear it.'

'And the house?' Lee asked curiously. 'What did you intend to do with that?'

'A son of one of my foresters is getting married soon; I would probably have the chalet repaired and let him live there.'

'You wouldn't pull it down, then?' Somehow the answer to the question seemed suddenly very important.

There was a slight frown on his forehead as he looked at her, then he smiled reassuringly. '*Nein*, I wouldn't have it pulled down. It has too much history, too many memories for that.'

So he, too, had sensed, as she had done, how the house must have looked in happier times. Lee gave a little sigh of relief. 'I'm glad you feel like that.'

He raised a quizzical eyebrow. 'Does that mean you will consider selling to me?'

Lee looked rather wistfully back at the decrepit house. 'I don't really have any choice, do I?' she said practically. 'No one is going to look at it as a paying proposition or an investment, and it would cost the earth to have the house modernised and repaired to sell as a home. So, really, I suppose I'm lucky that it even has a nuisance value.' Then she realised just how cross Richard would have been if he had heard her admit that much, so she added hastily, 'But I shall have to have an independent valuation, of course.'

'Of course,' Max von Rejstoven agreed gravely, but there was something in his voice that made Lee glance quickly up at him to find his blue eyes alight with amusement.

Laughingly she admitted, 'That did sound awfully pompous, didn't it?'

'But also extremely businesslike. Who advised you to say it? Your father?'

Tilting her head to one side, Lee looked up at him rather roguishly. 'What makes you believe I didn't think of it myself?'

He laughed, a deep, masculine laugh, and cupped her chin in his hand. 'Because you're far too young and beautiful to have your head stuffed full of legal jargon. So who told you?'

Flushing with pleasure at his compliment, Lee said, 'It was Richard. He's my fiancé. He's a lawyer and he gave me a whole list of do's and don'ts before I came. He made me ...' She broke off as she saw that the smile had suddenly gone from his face.

'Your fiancé?' he said slowly. 'But you aren't wearing a ring.'

'No, we're not officially engaged, you see. It's—it's just sort of understood.' Lee faltered slightly under Max von Reistoven's gaze, then added with a rush, 'That's why the legacy seemed such a godsend. It meant that we wouldn't have to wait any longer—we could get married straight away.' She stopped as he stood up and looked away from her, back towards the Chalet Alpenrose.

'So that was why you were in such a hurry,' he murmured. 'Why didn't your—fiancé come with you?'

'He couldn't get away. He's involved in an important case.' Lee, too, had scrambled to her feet.

'Have you seen everything you wish to see?' he asked politely, his laughing mood of a few moments ago seeming to have disappeared altogether.

'Yes, thank you.'

'Then I think you should be getting back to your hotel. Where are you staying?'

'At the Hotel Erlenbach.'

'Ah, yes. I'm sure the proprietor there will be able to recommend a valuer to you. I expect you feel the same as I in that the sooner the deal goes through the better?'

'Yes, of course.' He helped her to mount the chestnut and Lee watched him with a puzzled expression as he mounted his own big black animal. Why had his manner towards her changed so abruptly? She had been enjoying his company, been glad that it was he who wanted to buy the property because she felt at ease with him and had started to like him for himself, but then a coldness seemed to have suddenly grown between them, a coldness of his making, so that now he was behaving only as a polite acquaintance.

He led her along the track leading down into the valley until they came to a fork, one path leading up the other side of the hill to the distant walls of the castle, the other continuing back down into the village.

'This way will take you to the road leading into Ausbach,' he told her, indicating the latter route. 'Mine is the other path.' He hesitated. 'Perhaps I should stress again how old and—and senile your great-uncle became in the last few years. He rebuffed every offer of help and behaved as if he were being persecuted. I'm sure that Herr Kreuz will tell you more of this when you see him, but I would be grateful if you would hear what he has to say with an open mind.' He looked at her searchingly. 'Will you try to do that, Fräulein Summers?'

Rather taken aback by the urgency in his voice, Lee could only reply, 'Why, yes, of course I will.'

He nodded. 'Good, then I will wish you *auf wiedersehen* for the present.' He raised his riding-crop in salute and dug his heels into his horse to send it cantering up the hill.

After returning the chestnut to his stable, Lee drove back to the hotel and found Herr Gruber most helpful in giving her the name of a valuer, in fact he luckily had the address of one who spoke English on his desk, so she was able to telephone straightaway. When she explained that she was only a visitor to Austria, the valuer was more than helpful and agreed to go to the chalet the very next day and let her have his report the day after that. Pleased with her success but rather tired and achey after her unaccustomed exercise, she decided to go to bed early to read, but just as she was on her way upstairs after dinner, Herr Gruber told her that there was a phone call for her. Quickly she ran down to the little telephone booth and picked up the receiver.

'Richard? Is that you, darling?'

There was a pause before a masculine voice said slowly, 'I'm sorry to disappoint you, *Fräulein*, but this is Max von Reistoven. Did you have any success with a valuer?'

'Yes, I did.' Quickly Lee explained the position.

'I see.' He seemed to deliberate for a moment, then amazed her by saying, 'If you have nothing planned for tomorrow perhaps you would allow me to show you a little of the Tyrol? You haven't been up into the high mountains yet, have you?'

'Why, no. But really, Herr von Reistoven, you don't have to go to that trouble. I'll be . . .'

'It will be my pleasure, *Fräulein*. I will pick you up at—shall we say nine-thirty?'

'Th-thank you, that will be fine.' In rather a daze Lee put down the receiver and went up to her room to prepare for bed. Her book forgotten, she lay in the darkened room and watched the bars of moonlight that filtered through the windows. It had been a day of mixed events, mixed emotions; her delight on first seeing the perfect picture the chalet made and her disappointment at its condition; her enjoyment of Max von Reistoven's company and her bewilderment when he had seemed to change towards her when she had told him of her engagement. Was it because he disapproved of her being here alone? Or was it because he had foreseen all sorts of legal wrangling when he found out that Richard was a lawyer? Whatever it was, it would appear that he had decided to overlook it or he wouldn't have asked her out tomorrow. To the high mountains, he had said, and Lee was still thinking of the mountains and of Max von Reistoven when she drifted off to sleep.

The big grey Mercedes pulled up in the forecourt of the hotel promptly next morning and Lee went rather hesitantly down the steps to meet him, unsure of what to expect. But she needn't have worried, for Max greeted her with a friendly smile and courteously made sure she was comfortable and had everything she needed before driving off. He took her deep into the Alps, along side roads through toyland villages that had not yet been overrun by tourists, driving quite fast, but with skill and confidence so that Lee felt no alarm as the powerful car took the hairpin bends in its stride.

At length he pulled up in a car park near a cable-car station at the foot of one of the highest peaks.

'Are we really going up in that?' The cables that held the car looked awfully fragile as they stretched out into space towards the summit.

He smiled. 'It's quite safe.' He led her to the small queue of people waiting for the car to come down and Lee became aware of how people turned their heads to look at them. Max was wearing a tan safari-style suit that, despite its well-cut casualness, didn't detract from his authoritative, carelessly arrogant manner, and Lee supposed it was this that made people move out of his way to let him pass and the ticket seller to speak so deferentially.

The ride in the cable-car was one that Lee would never forget. At first it was rather nerve-racking to find oneself suspended in mid-air, but soon the breath-taking panorama set out around her made her forget the sheer drop below. After they had rattled noisily into the cable-station on the mountain top they wandered round the walks that had been cut out of the rock-face. In one area an alpine garden had been planted with edelweiss and other rock plants which climbed their colourful way among the nooks and crevices of the bare brown rock.

Suddenly a thick mist shut out the sun and enveloped them in greyness. Hastily Lee pulled on the sweater that she had brought with her. 'Ugh, this mist is damp! I can feel the moisture on my face and hair.'

'It isn't mist,' Max told her with a smile. 'You're standing in the middle of a cloud. Come, I'll show you.'

He led her to where a part of the mountain jutted out from the face. A wall had been built for the safety of tourists so that they could look across the valley to the precipitous slopes of the other alps all around them.

'Watch. Soon you'll be able to see through the cloud.'

He moved closer to her, his hand resting lightly on her shoulder as he indicated the point where she was to watch. His hand felt warm and strong and it was a few minutes before she realised that the cloud had begun to shred and then, through a hole that slowly cleared, she saw the sun shining *below* them, and deep down in the valley a tiny red-roofed village with its shiny black upside-down radish of a church spire and a river that wound its way between the houses. It was like looking at a miniature landscape painting—a painting framed in grey cotton wool.

A slight breeze chased the cloud away to settle on other mountain tops and Lee turned to speak to Max, but her voice died in her throat as she found him watching her, a rather pensive expression in his eyes that were as intensely blue as the mountain sky. The expression changed as soon as she looked at him and he suggested they have lunch in the hotel built on a nearby plateau. Here there was a huge dining-room with lines of wooden tables and benches. Max ordered soup for them, but as they hadn't brought a picnic lunch Lee rather thought that a bowl of soup wouldn't be very filling; however, the waitress brought a tray with a huge tureen of thick, hot vegetable soup with two bowls and spoons, and while Max was serving this, she came back with a basket piled high with chunks of French bread and a mound of butter pats. The coolness in the cloud had made them both hungry, but it was more than their combined appetites could do to empty the tureen.

'Gosh, do they always give you this much?' Lee asked as she laid her spoon down at last.

'It's mostly for the hikers and climbers, so they make it very thick and nourishing. You get the best soup in Austria in the mountain hotels.'

The second peak they visited was by funicular railway this time; a small, noisy engine that pulled three carriages of tourists as it chugged its way slowly up the precipitous zig-zag track, stopping at tiny halts to pick up hikers who had given up and who flopped gratefully into the empty seats. It was quite late when they finally descended from this mountain and Lee thought that Max would take her back to her hotel, but instead he drove her to an inn, a very old Tyrolean building with a fretwork of beams supporting the ceiling and tables with red and white chequered cloths set around a cleared space in the middle of the lamplit room. They ate a delicious meal and Lee tried hard to remember the names of the dishes, but couldn't, and drank wine that made her feel relaxed and tell Max all about her life in England when he asked her. A compère came into the cleared space and to Lee's delight announced an exhibition of folk entertainment.

There were dancers in ornate versions of the peasant

dress that Lee had seen worn by girls in Ausbach. They had full dirndl skirts and beautifully embroidered hand-made blouses that made Lee decide she had to buy one before she left Austria; but the prettiest part of their costumes were the white lace headdresses that framed their faces so becomingly. In between the dances there were displays of various types of Tyrolean skills. Everyone enjoyed the race between a man sawing through a log of wood and another chopping his way through, and joined in the cheers when the man with the axe finally won. But Lee found herself fascinated by the demonstration of flag-throwing by two men in traditional male peasant dress of Tyrolean hat, soft, full-sleeved shirt and short grey leather trousers—*Lederhosen*, Max told her they were called—and long grey socks with buckled shoes.

The flags, of Austria and the Tyrol, were thrown high into the air, twisting and turning as they fell, only to be skilfully caught and tossed up again to pass each other in mid-air and be caught by the other man. The silken colours in the flags glowed warmly in the dimmed room and the only noise was the whirr and flap of the billowing ensigns. Then suddenly they were still, the whole room hushed and quiet. From outside, on the slope of the mountain, there came clearly and unmistakably the sound of an alpine horn, its deep, melancholy note echoing and re-echoing through the mountains until it faded into infinity. Lee sat there, strangely moved by the simple and ancient ceremony and it was several moments before she could bring herself to look at Max. He was watching her with a strangely gentle look in his eyes, and she flushed as she realised how an evening that had seemed so wonderful and new to her would be only commonplace to him. This tall, enigmatic man belonged to his castle set among the crags, and Lee—he was being kind to her because she was a stranger in his country, knew no one, couldn't even speak the language—nothing more. Then he stood up and politely helped her to her feet. The show was over, it was time to go.

Only a dim pool of light lit the entrance to the hotel when Max walked her to the door. Putting out her hand, Lee looked up at him and said sincerely, 'Thank you. It's been a really wonderful day.'

Max took her hand in his, but instead of shaking it he raised it briefly to his lips, then astounded her by saying, 'You know, *Fräulein*, if I had been your fiancé the engagement would be very official—and very, very short!' His eyes held hers for a moment, then he turned precipitately and strode back to his car.

The valuer's report was waiting for her after breakfast the next morning and Lee was pleased to find that he had put a value on the Chalet Alpenrose that was a little under the offer that Max had made for it. So the solicitor had been right; it had been a fair price. Thinking of the solicitor made her impatient for his return, so she drove round to his office where the secretary told her that Herr Kreuz would be back later that day. Lee made an appointment for three o'clock and passed the time in between visiting a nearby town famed for its woodcarvers. She spent an enjoyable couple of hours looking round the shops and buying presents for her parents, and a rather expensive carved panel which she told herself was for Richard, but which she couldn't resist, then had lunch in a pretty open-air restaurant overlooking a small lake before driving back to Ausbach to keep her appointment.

Herr Kreuz was a thin, elderly man with a small moustache and glasses that he kept looking over the top of, but he greeted Lee warmly and soon got down to business. Besides the chalet and land, Lee was surprised to hear that her great-uncle had also left her a small insurance policy.

'You will have read in my letter of the offer that has been made for the chalet,' the solicitor went on. 'When you have seen the property it may be that . . .'

'But I have seen it,' Lee interrupted him. 'I went there the other day and saw the state the place was in, so I got an independent valuation on it.' She pulled the report from her bag and gave it to him.

Herr Kreuz pushed his glasses back on his nose and read it through carefully. 'Who gave you the name of this company, *Fräulein*?'

'Herr Gruber at the hotel. It tallies quite closely with Herr von Reistoven's offer, so I don't see . . .'

'But how did you know that it was Herr von Reistoven who had made the offer?' the solicitor asked sharply.

'I met him quite by accident when I was going to the chalet and he told me. I said I would accept his offer if the valuation was satisfactory.'

Herr Kreuz looked at her in some perturbation. 'You seem to be in a great hurry, Fräulein Summers.'

'Well, there doesn't seem to be any point in delaying, does there? I only have a limited time at my disposal.'

'But you don't know all the circumstances. Your great-uncle was not on the best of terms with Max von Reistoven. It may be that he would not have wanted you to sell to him.'

Lee looked at the solicitor in some astonishment. 'But you told me about the offer in the first place!'

'I was duty bound to do so, but I intended telling you all the circumstances before you made up your mind. You see . . .'

'It isn't necessary to go into details, Herr Kreuz, I already know that Uncle Howard regarded Max von

Reistoven as his enemy, that he had a persecution complex about it.'

The solicitor looked at her over his glasses, his eyebrows raised. 'Who told you this?'

'Herr von Reistoven himself. He was very open about it. My great-uncle didn't specifically state in his will that I wasn't to sell to him, did he?'

'No, you are to dispose of the property as you wish.'

'Then please will you draw up the necessary papers for the sale to Herr von Reistoven?' Still the solicitor seemed to hesitate and Lee added rather impatiently, 'Who else would I sell it to? Obviously no one would want it as it is, and I don't have the capital for repairs and modernisation even if I wanted to keep the house.'

For a long moment the solicitor continued to look at her, then he shook his head with a sigh. 'Very well, Fräulein Summers, it shall be as you wish. I will contact Herr von Reistoven and the contract should be ready to be signed within a few days.'

He kept her only a little longer and then Lee found herself back in the sunshine again. Slowly she walked back to her car, but didn't drive off straight away. She supposed she had behaved rather abruptly towards the solicitor, but somewhere deep inside she had a feeling of unrest, an increasing urge to have the business settled and get back to England, to her own familiar surroundings and to Richard. It wasn't homesickness, rather an inner fear that if she stayed too long in this beautiful country she might not want to go back. She looked at the little street of houses, alive with the rich colours of ancient wood, of wall paintings, of flowers, and, at the end of the road, the green wooded slopes rising to high granite peaks, and above everything the intense blue of the summer sky. Remembering the noisy, choking city streets she had left so recently, Lee realised there was no comparison—none at all!

The air was very still and hot; there was no breeze to sway the flowers that grew beneath the crosses of stone and ornate iron that dotted the little churchyard on the slope behind the church. Butterflies settled undisturbed and ladybirds climbed their slow way over neat paths between the graves. On a wooden bench set under the shade of a tree an old man rested, apparently asleep, his head cupped in gnarled hands that leaned heavily on a stick. In an area of starkly new headstones, some only just beginning to weather, Lee found the one she sought—a plain stone bearing her great-uncle's name, 'Howard Canning', with the dates of his birth and death, nothing more.

After arranging the flowers she had brought with her, she stood for a time looking at the stone and wondering about this man whom she hardly remembered but who had thought enough of her to leave her all he possessed. He, too, had been young once, had stepped boldly out to meet whatever life had to offer him. She hoped that he had lived it to the full, enough to make up for his illness in the last few years. Turning to go away, she almost jumped out of her skin when she found that the old man who had been sitting on the bench had come quietly up behind her.

'Fräulein Summers.' The words were more a statement than a question. 'I have been waiting to see if you would come here, if you cared enough about my old friend to seek out his last resting place.' The old man spoke excellent English and his rather rheumy eyes were very much alive in his weathered face. 'My name is Johann Staffler and your uncle lived with me in Ausbach until his death. That was after he was forced out of the Chalet Alpenrose, of course,' he added deliberately.

'Forced out?' Lee found herself staring into his eyes as if mesmerised.

'Yes.' He turned and slowly went to the seat under the tree, Lee following him. 'Herr Kreuz, too, is an old friend. He told me that you were only interested in selling the estate and getting the money, that you did not want to hear anything about the details of Howard Canning's death. But Howard often spoke of you with great affection and I did not believe he could mean nothing to you, so I decided to sit here and wait to see if you would come. If you did not ...' he shrugged, 'then I would know that Herr Kreuz was right. But you did come, so I know that you did care about my old friend.'

'What do you mean, "the details of his death"? And why was he forced to leave the chalet?' Lee asked in some bewilderment. 'I thought he died of a heart attack?'

'That was the official medical reason, yes,' Herr Staffler agreed. 'But in reality he was virtually driven into his grave by the measures that were brought to bear on him to give up the Alpenrose estate.'

'But I don't understand. What measures? And who brought them against him?'

The old man looked at her. 'Why, Max von Reistoven, of course.'

Lee stared at him; was this the kind of thing that Max had warned her about? Asked her to hear with an open mind? Carefully she said, 'I know that Uncle Howard had been unwell and unable to look after the estate properly. Perhaps he imagined that Herr von Reistoven was treating him unfairly ...'

'Imagined!' Herr Staffler almost barked the word out. 'What are you trying to say—that his mind was gone? Bah! You are as bad as the others. Just because a man's body is winding down it does not mean that his mind is too. Howard Canning's brain was as alert and intelligent as it ever was. But what is the point of telling you? You have already made up your mind to believe what they want you to believe,' the old man grumbled bitterly. 'You don't care after all; don't care that he went through years of physical hardships and worry because of what the von Reistovens did to him.'

Lee found that her fingernails were digging into her palms. Numbly she said, 'I think you'd better tell me all about it.'

Herr Staffler had stood up to leave, but now he sat down again. 'Very well. When Howard married Erika von Reistoven ...' he began, then, at Lee's start of surprise, added, 'You did not know this?'

'No,' Lee said slowly. 'No, I didn't.'

'Yes, she married him against her family's wishes, but she had been given the Chalet Alpenrose as her dowry in the will of Max von Reistoven's grandfather. She was only a cousin, of course, or some such, or the dowry would have been much more. However, they lived there comfortably enough until she died, but then, almost immediately after the funeral, Max von Reistoven told your uncle that he would have to leave, that the Alpenrose estate had been given only for his wife's lifetime, as was the annuity to help run it, and reverted to the von Reistovens on her death. But Howard Canning had always understood that the estate was his wife's to dispose of as she wished. He consulted lawyers and began a legal battle that drained all his resources, leaving nothing with which to maintain the estate, and so giving Max von Reistoven another excuse for trying to take it from him.'

Herr Staffler thumped his stick angrily. 'But that wasn't all he tried to do to get Howard out. He refused to let motor-driven vehicles use the access road from the village so your uncle had to walk all the way whenever he wanted something—and that in the depths of winter! He even dammed the stream so that the chalet was without water. In the end Howard Canning's life became intolerable and he could not go on living there, but he never gave up—he was still fighting for his rights when he died.'

'But why?' Lee asked in perplexity. 'Why should Max von Reistoven want to turn an old man out of his home? He has so much, why should he want more?'

'Because that is the kind of people the Von Reistovens are,' the old man said vehemently. 'They will not part with an inch of their property. What they have, they hold!'

'But if he really believed that the chalet belonged to him, why should he offer to buy it from me?' Lee said reasonably.

'It is the easiest way to get it back, and cheaper than fighting more law-suits,' Herr Staffler told her grimly. 'He could pay you off and that would be the end of it.'

Pay her off! Lee sat back on the bench and felt a tide of revulsion sweep over her. Was that what Max had been doing? Showing her the chalet himself, taking her out, being attentive towards her, even paying her compliments, while telling her a lying version of the truth so that she would feel that she could trust him? And she had trusted him, completely. Talking to him as a friend, as someone she liked. How he must have been laughing to himself at her gullibility! she thought bitterly. He had probably only taken her out to keep her away from Ausbach and such a meeting as this until he was sure of her. Sure that she would eagerly accept his offer and go happily back to England congratulating herself on her luck. And how she had played into his hands! Telling him what the money would mean to her, while all the time he had been determined to get the land into his own hands to keep his precious estate intact; had been so obsessed with getting it back that he had even hounded an old man to death to do so. A great surge of anger and bitterness formed like a cold, hard ball inside her and she resolved there and then that Max von Reistoven would pay for what he had done to her uncle—and for what he had done to her, too, she vowed grimly.

Abruptly she stood up and said to Herr Staffler, 'I think I'd better go and talk to Herr Kreuz again. Will you come with me?'

'Of course, of course.' The old man scrambled agilely to his feet and hurried along beside her, a pleased expression in his eyes.

They passed Howard Canning's grave again and Lee paused to ask, 'Why wasn't he buried next to his wife?'

Her companion said sourly, 'She was a Von Reistoven; they buried her in the chapel in the castle. But they didn't want Howard, even when he was dead he wasn't good enough to join her!'

CHAPTER THREE

ONCE again Lee sat and looked at the Chalet Alpenrose, but in what different circumstances from the first time. Now she could feel the hard lump of the keys in the pocket of her jeans and knew that she faced the mammoth task of putting the house in good enough repair to attract an outside offer for it, for she was now just as determined as her great-uncle had been not to let Max von Reistoven get his hands on the estate. The previous day, after her meeting with Herr Staffler, they had had a long conference in the solicitor's office and the two men had promised to help her all they could. The Three Musketeers! Lee thought with irony—a feeble old man, an elderly solicitor and a twenty-one-year-old girl! But already things were happening. Herr Kreuz had made a deal with the farmer, Herr Schneider, and arranged for her to receive a small rent and the use of the chestnut gelding in exchange for grazing a herd of cows and the horse in her meadows. Her meadows! Lee smiled to herself; she still hadn't got used to the idea that the chalet was really hers. Perhaps that was why it had been so easy to agree to sell it.

There was no fear of the animals straying as they moved through the lush, long grass; the fences all bordered on to the von Reistoven estates and they had been well maintained. Well, she had that to thank Max for if nothing else. Lee crossed to the house and this time ventured into the ground floor part, but the doors leading into it hadn't been opened for ages and she had to scrape away a build-up of soil and weeds with an old piece of metal she found before she could get the heavy doors open. Once inside she was relieved to find, not rotting hay and dank earth as she had expected, but a fairly clean stone floor with piles of cut logs stored against one wall and in another corner two lines of empty wine racks, their bottles used long since. A flight of stairs ran up from this large store room to a trapdoor in what must be the floor of the kitchen and which she hadn't noticed on her first visit here with Max. Probably because the floor was too filthy, she thought with distaste, knowing that one of her first tasks would be to clean it.

The sound of a car engine brought her out into the open again and she went forward to meet Herr Kreuz and a builder he had brought with him to give an estimate for repairing the roof. Lee showed them round and then went to stand on the balcony with Herr Kreuz while the builder measured up and made notes on an ever-growing list of repairs.

'It is very beautiful here,' the solicitor commented. 'This is one of the best views in the area, and we are not short of wonderful views in Austria.'

Lee smiled. 'Perhaps someone will buy the place for the view, then.'

Herr Kreuz turned to look at her intently. 'You realise that you are taking on more than the repair of the chalet? You are also taking on Max von Reistoven, and he can be a formidable adversary.'

'Yes, I know. But if what Herr Staffler told me is true then he is also a liar and a cheat and ought to be shown up for what he is.'

'My dear Fräulein Summers, please don't do anything hasty,' he said hurriedly. 'You have only Herr Staffler's word that these things happened. True, he and your great-uncle also told me and I tried to help them, but old men can be inclined to exaggerate, you know. You must make no accusations without evidence to support them, or you might find yourself in serious trouble. The von Reistovens are very powerful.'

'Then all the more reason for showing them up for what they are!' Lee exclaimed angrily.

Herr Kreuz looked at her worriedly. '*Fräulein*, please promise me that you won't do anything rash.'

Lee appreciated his concern for her and made the promise rather unwillingly; she would dearly have loved to tell Max von Reistoven just what she thought of him. It was unlikely, however, that she would ever see him again, for Herr Kreuz had written to his solicitors telling them that she had decided not to accept his offer after all. It gave her immense satisfaction to imagine his reaction when he heard *that* piece of news.

How angry he would be that all the time he had spent buttering her up had been wasted, and now he was further than he had ever been from getting the Alpenrose estate.

The builder had finished his inspection and was able to give a rough figure there and then, but to Lee's dismay the insurance money that Howard Canning had left wasn't enough to cover it. There followed a session of hard bargaining between the three of them and at the end of that time Lee found that she had committed herself to redecorating the chalet and to helping as much as she could, so cutting the builder's costs to a price she could afford. Just how she had agreed to this she didn't quite know, and it wasn't until she was back in her hotel room that the full import of what she had done hit her. The builder had promised to start work straightaway, but even so it might take them a couple of weeks to finish and she wouldn't be able to complete her part until after they had gone. But she had only taken two weeks' leave from her office!

Slumping down on the bed, Lee tried to think of ways and means round the problem and at length came to the only sensible conclusion; she would just have to write to her firm and tell them that she had resigned and wouldn't be coming back. That way she wouldn't have to worry if the builders took longer than anticipated and she would be able to work in her own time without having to rush. Just what Richard was going to say to this when only two days ago she had told him all was going well, she hated to think, and it was with some trepidation that she rang him after dinner that evening.

'Hallo, darling.' His voice sounded tinny and far away. 'How are things going? Have you signed the contract yet?'

'Well, no, I haven't. You see, Richard, I . . .'

'Then tell your solicitor chappie to hurry up. I'm missing you.'

'Richard, are you really?'

'Of course. I wish you could have been in court today. I cross-examined one of the minor witnesses and the chief counsel actually said he was pleased with the way I handled it.'

'Why, Richard, that's marvellous! But there's something I want to tell you,' Lee said urgently. 'I've decided not to sell to Herr von Reistoven after all. In fact I—I've decided to give up my job and stay here while the house is being repaired.'

'What did you say, Lee? I don't think I could have heard you properly. It sounded as if you were going to give up your job.'

'Yes, that's right. You see, lots of things have cropped up and I just have to stay here to sort them out,' she added rather desperately, knowing exactly what Richard was thinking. 'I'll write and tell you all about it, but it might be several weeks before I come home.'

'You can't possibly give up your job. It's madness,' he rejoined angrily. 'Lee, I won't let you.'

'Well, I'm afraid you can't stop me, Richard, because I've already sent my resignation,' she retorted. Then, more gently, 'Look, darling, I do know what I'm doing and you'll understand when you get my letter. And we'll probably get more for the property this way than by selling to Herr von Reistoven.'

There was an ominous silence on the line and then Richard said coldly, 'Very well, Lee, if you've made up your mind without waiting to consult me there's nothing I can do about it, but I think you're being very foolish. Giving up your job just to make sure some repairs are carried out properly—it's absurd!'

He refused to be placated and told her again that

she was being ridiculous, until Lee said rather abruptly that she would write and put the phone down.

She could understand how Richard felt, she supposed she would feel the same if it had been the other way round, but he might at least have waited to pass judgment until he had received her letter. But what a hard letter it was to write, as she found when she sat down to do it. How could she make Richard see that she must take up her great-uncle's cause, with all that might entail? At length she finished, but reading it through she had doubts that Richard would ever really understand why she hadn't just sold the chalet and come home again. He would have told her to let old feuds die and to leave well alone. Lee sighed; a very practical man was Richard—she doubted if he had ever hated anyone in his life.

On Sunday mornings everything came to a halt in Ausbach as the villagers dressed in their best and made their way to the little church. Along with Herr Gruber and several other guests from the hotel, Lee joined the throng, taking her place in a pew on the left-hand side of the church. For a moment she glanced across towards the front pews on the other side of the aisle and found herself staring straight into Max von Reistoven's cold blue eyes. He stood head and shoulders above everyone else in the church and Lee instantly recognised the look on his face; he was furiously angry!

The service in the small but elaborately decorated church, alive with superb baroque architecture and magnificent woodcarving on screen and pulpit, was not a long one, but Lee found that she was hardly listening, merely standing up or kneeling when everyone else did so. She could see little of Max, but whenever she did catch a glimpse of him he was always looking, stony-faced, towards the front of the church. Eyes seemed to bore into her back and she could hear whispering behind her under cover of the organ music. She had dressed carefully in a grey suit and coral-coloured blouse, but there were several women in brighter clothes, so she knew that it couldn't be her appearance that was causing so much comment. She could only suppose that the village grapevine had been busy and that everyone knew who she was and that she had refused to sell the chalet to Max. A juicy bit of news for all the village gossips, she thought wryly.

At last the service was over and everyone trooped outside again, but Lee didn't join the rest of the guests in their saunter back to the hotel, instead standing to one side to let the worshippers pass. Among the last, Max at length came through the arched doorway with an elegant middle-aged woman who stopped to talk to the parson. He stepped aside to wait, but then he saw Lee and strode purposefully towards her. Lee awaited him with cold defiance. She had a score to settle with Max von Reistoven!

'Why have you turned down my offer?' he demanded at once.

Lee looked up at him artlessly. 'Oh, didn't the solicitor tell you? I've changed my mind.'

'But why, *Fräulein*? You were perfectly happy with my offer the last time I saw you. Have people been telling you things, because if so . . .'

'Things?' Lee said innocently, opening her eyes wide. 'What things?'

He stopped, eyeing her suspiciously. 'Just why have you decided not to sell to me, *Fräulein*? If it's more money . . .'

'Good heavens, it isn't that. I've decided to turn the place into a camping site, with a special area set aside for caravans, and I'm having cabins built in the woods especially for honeymoon couples. So romantic, don't you think? Oh, yes, I almost forgot, there's going to be a disco in the ground floor of the house and a jazz festival every Saturday,' she finished with malicious enjoyment at the look on Max's face.

His jaw tightened. 'Do you think I believe a word of that? You promised to listen to Herr Kreuz with an open mind, but obviously you prefer to believe him rather than me.'

'And Herr Staffler,' Lee broke in coldly. 'Don't forget that there's someone else who knows what you did to my great-uncle. Trying to take his home away from him, hounding him until he died!'

Max lunged forward and caught hold of her wrist so tightly that it hurt. 'Gott in himmel! You little idiot!' His eyes were as cold as steel as he glared at her. 'How can you listen to that old fool? He's as twisted and bitter as your great-uncle was. Don't be blinded by what he tells you. I tried to help Herr Canning, offered to let him live at the Schloss ...'

'Oh, don't go on lying,' Lee said in disgust. 'I'm not naïve and trusting any longer. I've learnt the truth about you now and I think you're utterly despicable! So greedy that you can't even let an old man live out his days in peace. You're not fit to ...'

But suddenly Max had pulled her towards him, the grip on her wrist tightening so that she winced with pain. His eyes blazed so furiously that she thought he was going to shake her, but he said savagely, 'Mein Gott, if you were a man I'd knock you down for saying that!'

'Yes, you'd like that, wouldn't you?' Lee taunted. 'Brute force is all your kind understand. Trample the weak underfoot just so that you get your precious bit of land back and ...' She stopped abruptly as she saw a look in his eyes that was far more dangerous than anger or rage. She had gone too far, and heaven knows what

Max would have done to her if a puzzled voice behind him hadn't said his name at that moment. Immediately he let go of her wrist and turned to place his broad back between Lee and the middle-aged woman with whom he had come out of the church. The woman asked him a question, obviously referring to Lee.

'*Niemand bedevtend*,' he replied. '*Nur ein Tourist.*'

Lee's face was rather pale except for two spots of colour high on her cheekbones when she got back to the hotel. The proprietor was seated at the reception desk and Lee went across to him.

'Herr Gruber, what does *Niemand bedevtend. Nur ein Tourist* mean?' she asked him, repeating the phrase Max had used.

'It means, No one of importance. Merely a tourist,' he told her, and was surprised to see the look of anger that came into her hazel eyes. So that was what Max von Reistoven thought of her, was it? Well, one day she was going to make him apologise for that—preferably grovelling on his knees!

Sounds of hammering and sawing filled the valley as the builder and his men started the repair work on the chalet. The smell of newly-cut timber filled Lee's nostrils as she watched them erect scaffolding to hold up the roof while the rotten wall timbers were replaced with new ones. The men seemed happy enough, laughing and whistling as they worked, and Lee wished she could understand their Austrian dialect, but then a general roar of laughter made her think that perhaps it was just as well she couldn't; a gang of men working together were the same the world over! She spent the day working against time to clear the ground floor of the house so that building materials and tools could be stored there and locked away at night. By the time the men left and she was able to lock up she was thoroughly dirty and had to scrub herself and wash her hair twice before she felt clean again.

During the course of the next morning a lorry load of timber arrived and was stacked at a convenient distance from the house as this was to be used to repair the balcony and the steps leading up to it. The men threw the broken and rotten wood down to the ground to be disposed of, and Lee somehow found herself with an unwieldy scythe in her hand and, after only a few minutes' demonstration, expected to clear a large area of long grass at the back of the house so that there wouldn't be any danger of catching the field alight when they lit a bonfire to burn the old wood. She started work rather nervously, half afraid of cutting her toes off, but got the hang of it with practice, although making slow progress.

Soon her arms felt as if they were coming out of the sockets and her legs ached unbearably. She stopped, panting, to take five minutes' rest, but knowing that the men were watching her, she gritted her teeth and picked up the scythe again. The horrible thing felt like lead in her hands that were starting to blister. She thought of how she could have been back home in London planning her wedding to Richard by now if it hadn't been for that beast Max von Reistoven. Thinking of him made her swing the scythe viciously and she found that it helped a lot. So with every swing she thought of all the things she'd like to do to him, and the area was cleared far more quickly than she had expected.

Rather proudly she went over to tell the builder that he could now build his bonfire, but after a conversation in his broken English and her very broken German gathered that she was expected to do that too. She looked in dismay at the mouldy wood and then at what had been an expensive shirt and jeans. She sighed:

at least she'd learnt enough to bring a scarf for her hair today. All afternoon she dragged the heavy timbers across the field and built an extremely ragged-looking bonfire. Before long her clothes and arms were stained and filthy and there was a large smear of dirt across her face where she had wiped away the perspiration that ran down her forehead. The workmen went home, but Lee was determined to finish stacking the rubbish that day, so went on to add the last few pieces to the pile.

She had just gaspingly lugged another wall timber on to the stack and turned to go for another when she looked up to see a horseman astride a big black stallion riding easily up to her. Max reined in the horse only a few feet away and looked her up and down slowly, taking in every detail, then lifted one mobile eyebrow.

'I had heard that the British were enthusiastic—how do you put it—do-it-yourself experts, but I hadn't realised that it extended to Austrian chalets. I must congratulate you, *Fräulein*, you seem to be quite throwing yourself into your work.'

Lee glared at him. 'Don't you know you're trespassing?' she countered, deciding to ignore his sarcasm.

'So I am.' But as he spoke he dismounted and set the horse loose to graze. He came across and stood, tall and powerful, just in front of her. 'So why don't you throw me out?' he taunted her.

Lee stared up at him for a moment and then turned her back on him to walk away, but he came to walk along beside her.

'Aren't you going to show me how the work is progressing?'

'Certainly not! Why should I?'

'Well, it is my house,' he said in the tones of one who is patiently trying to explain something to a simpleton.

Swinging round to face him, Lee retorted angrily,

'That's a lie and you know it! My great-uncle had a perfect right to this house.'

'Had he? You know that for a fact, do you? You've read all the papers in the case, checked my grandfather's will that entailed it originally, and all the other relevant documents? You know without any doubt that you're the rightful owner, do you?' he asked sharply, his eyes watching her intently as she tried to mask the dismay his questions had aroused in her.

Biting her lip, Lee turned away. It was quite true that she hadn't done any of those things herself, but Herr Kreuz must have done so for Uncle Howard and found them sufficient proof, or they would never have had a chance in court. Max was just trying to undermine her resolve by putting doubts in her mind. Bending down, she picked up a couple of planks to take over to the bonfire.

'Here, let me do that for you,' Max said at once, and went to take them from her.

'Take your hands away,' Lee said angrily. 'I can manage perfectly well and I certainly don't need your help!'

He stood back at once and went to lean against a tree trunk, his arms folded, as he nonchalantly watched her working. At length she couldn't stand his gaze any longer.

'Why don't you just go away?' she demanded, goaded into exasperation.

'But I'm enjoying myself,' he said mockingly. 'Tell me, does your fiancé approve of what you're doing?'

'Richard? Yes, of—of course.' She tried to sound positive, but was afraid he might have noticed her hesitation so added for good measure, 'He's a hundred per cent behind me. He doesn't like intimidation either.'

'Really?' Max's voice was heavy with irony. 'I should have thought that he was used to it.'

Lee dropped the planks and confronted him angrily. 'And just what is that supposed to mean?'

'Merely that anyone who is willing to take on a spoiled brat like you must be either a lovesick fool or a masochist.'

'Why, you ...!' Lee's hand, with all her strength behind it, came up to strike him across the face, but he had anticipated her action even before she had made it and caught her arm before it was anywhere near him. Struggling wildly, she tried to break away, but Max caught her other wrist and pulled her roughly against him so that she could feel his hard, lean body against her as she twisted to get free. Realising the futility of it, she stopped struggling to stand, quivering and helpless, but furious with rage, in front of him.

'You little tigress! I ought to do what that fiancé of yours should have done long ago and put you across my knee. A good spanking would do you the world of good.'

'As I've said before,' Lee replied sarcastically, 'brute force is your answer to everything. You're so big and you wield such power that I don't suppose anyone but Uncle Howard and I ever dared to stand up to you before, with the result that you think you can ride roughshod over everyone you meet, push aside anyone who gets in your way, and you couldn't care less if people get hurt in the process. Well, you can threaten and bully me all you want, but it won't get you anywhere, because I'm not afraid of you! I'm not a helpless old man to be kicked out of the way! And as for Richard—he's kind and gentle. Compared to him you're just a—a king-sized moron!'

Max had been watching her frowningly, his lips a thin line of anger during this tirade, but as she finished his look changed, his lips twitched and quite suddenly he began to laugh with genuine amusement. Irrationally this annoyed Lee more than ever and she again tried to break free, but he took both her wrists in his left hand and put his right under her chin so that she had to look at him. Hard blue eyes looked deep into her hazel ones.

'No,' he said in a strangely odd voice, 'I don't feel either kind or gentle towards you.'

For a moment longer he held her, then he bent and picked her up in his arms to carry her across to the Beetle and dump her unceremoniously in the driver's seat.

'Go home and get some rest. You've had enough for one day.' But whether he was referring to her work on the chalet or her argument with him, Lee didn't know.

She eyed him suspiciously, unwilling to leave while he was still there. He sensed her thoughts, for he said sarcastically, 'It's all right, *Fräulein*, you needn't be afraid. I'm hardly likely to burn down my own property.'

Angrily Lee started up the car and turned it in the direction of the village. She didn't even look to see if he was leaving, she wouldn't give him that much satisfaction. But as she drove back to the hotel her thoughts somehow returned to that moment when she had been held close to him. There had been a strange look in his eyes then that she couldn't understand and she had been afraid, but with a fascinated fear that had held her still, unable to prevent what he would do, not really wanting to. She shivered. God, how she wished she'd never met the man, never come to Austria. If only she hadn't listened to Richard everything could have been conducted by letter and she would never have got mixed up in old feuds, old hatreds. She tried to dismiss Max for what he was; a greedy, despotic brute of a man, but always she remembered how charming and— and downright *nice* he had been when they first met.

Next morning she got to the chalet early before the workmen arrived so that she could complete her unfinished task of the night before. But when she looked for the rest of the old wood it had disappeared. Her ragged pile of timbers had been pulled down and instead rebuilt into a neatly stacked bonfire with a wind tunnel full of small kindling. A note had been stuck on to a nail and when Lee took it down she read, 'Even morons sometimes have their uses—especially king-sized ones!'

CHAPTER FOUR

MOODILY Lee watched the workmen's lorry as it disappeared towards Ausbach in a small cloud of dust. The builder had just told her that an emergency had cropped up at another building site and he would need all his men for two days. It was now nearly a week since they had started repairing the chalet and the walls, stairs and balcony were all finished, but they had yet to complete the roof. Instead they had spread a big tarpaulin over the gap to keep out the weather. The results of her own handiwork could be seen in the newly painted window frames and shutters at the front of the house, the new glass panes gleaming in the sunlight. Lee understood that the builder had to answer the emergency, but she was worried about her growing hotel bill. Herr Gruber had taken her aside only the night before and explained that he had to increase his charges in the summer season, and asked her to decide whether she would prefer a smaller room without a bathroom.

As she sat and pondered over the problem Lee realised what a fool she had been. Why pay for a hotel room when she could live at the chalet? And if she lived on the premises she wouldn't need the Beetle to take her back and forth; if she did need to go into the village for supplies she could always hitch a lift with the workmen. The more she thought about it the more attractive the idea became, so within a few hours she had collected her luggage and checked out of the hotel, had bought herself a sleeping bag, camping stove and utensils, and enough food to last her for several days. These she left at the chalet while she drove the Beetle to the nearby town of Bergheim where she was able to leave it with an agent.

It took a long time to travel back by bus and an even longer time to tramp back to the chalet, but once there she felt a thrill of excitement; for the first time in her life she was going to spend the night alone in her own house. Come to think of it, it was going to be the first time she had ever spent a night so completely alone anywhere, but she pushed that thought resolutely aside and set to work to scrub out the chimney recess in the bedroom. When she had finished it smelt fresh and clean and she was able to spread her sleeping bag out in it without any fears of bugs or spiders sharing it with her.

Opening a couple of tins, she cooked herself an adequate meal on the little stove and rinsed the plates in the stream before making sure that all the doors were safely locked. It wasn't that she was nervous, she told herself firmly, but she lay awake for a long time listening to a gentle breeze lifting the corner of the tarpaulin and making it flap eerily against the wall, rather like the soft tread of footprints, and the cries of the screech owls as they hunted through the woods, before she eventually dropped into a restless sleep.

All the next morning she spent on cleaning out the rest of the bedroom, washing the walls and ceiling and scrubbing the floor. She had intended working on in the afternoon, but she suddenly found that she needed a break, to get right away from the chalet for a while. Taking the saddle that Herr Schneider had lent her, she caught the chestnut and was soon letting him have his head in a long gallop that took them far across the hill to the forest on the other side of the Schloss Reistoven. It was wonderful to feel the cool breeze in her hair after the heat of the valley and to sit astride the powerful animal as it carried her surely along, the ground flying beneath his hooves.

At length Lee reined in and bent to pat his neck in praise and gratitude. 'Well done, boy, that was fun!'

The horse whinnied as if in agreement and she laughed aloud, her voice echoing around her. For a while longer she continued to ride on, but the horse was lathered and she decided to cut through the forest below her and make her way back by a shorter route. They carried on easily down through the woods and she was just reaching the lower edge of the line of trees when the path she was following ran along beside a waterfall, swollen with melted snow, that plunged noisily out from the side of the rock face and jetted down into a narrow ravine before cascading on to the rocks below. Suddenly the horse pricked up his ears and snorted, stopping to paw the ground.

'What is it, boy? Does the waterfall frighten you?' Lee tried to urge him on, but the animal obstinately refused to move however much she encouraged him. Exasperated, she climbed from the saddle and tried to lead him past. 'Come on, old fellow, it won't hurt you.' She tugged on the bridle, but the horse merely put his ears back and neighed. It was then that Lee heard it From somewhere close at hand someone was shouting, a cry of desperation which she hadn't been able to hear before because of the noise of the waterfall. The shout came again and seemed unbelievably to be coming from inside the deep ravine. Quickly Lee went to the edge and looked over. Two small faces gazed hopefully up at her from a narrow ledge about eight feet down. One belonged to a dark-haired, freckle-faced little boy of about eight years old, the other to a floppy-eared, long-haired dog of decidedly mixed parentage who was held tightly in the boy's arms.

'Good heavens!' Lee exclaimed. 'How on earth did you get down there?'

'*Bitte, Fräulein. Mein Hundchen*...' Then realising that Lee had spoken in English, 'Please, my dog fall,' the boy managed.

'And I suppose you went down to get him and couldn't get back again.' Lee examined the side of the ravine carefully. It was an easy enough climb with both hands free, but it would be difficult carrying the boy; still, he looked pretty sensible, she decided. 'Hang on, I'm coming down,' she called. Cautiously she climbed down until she had a secure hand and foothold just above him. 'All right, pass me the dog.'

He did so somewhat reluctantly, but it took Lee only a moment to lift the whimpering animal on to solid ground. Then she went back down for the boy. Carefully she hoisted him on to her back.

'Hold tight and don't look down,' she instructed, hoping that he would understand.

In a very few minutes they were back on the path with the puppy joyously licking his young master's face. 'I call, I call, but no one come,' he said as relief gave way to tears. Bravely he wiped them on the back of his hand and sniffed loudly. Lee found a clean hanky in her pocket and handed it to him.

'Here, try this.'

'*Danke*.' He blew his nose hard and wiped his tear-stained little face, then politely offered the hanky back.

'Er—you keep it,' said Lee, looking at the screwed-up piece of linen. 'The puppy seems to be limping. Is he hurt?' Taking the animal from him, she examined it gently. 'He seems to have hurt his leg. I think we ought to take him to a vet.' Then seeing the look of incomprehension on the boy's face, she added, 'Animal doctor. For the dog.'

He seemed to understand, for he nodded eagerly, so Lee lifted the urchin up into the chestnut's saddle and climbed up behind him.

'What's your name? Name?' she repeated, pointing to him.

He grinned at her, revealing large gaps where his second teeth hadn't yet grown through. 'Rudi.'

'And I'm Lee Summers. And the dog?' Pointing to the puppy this time.

'*Das ist* Prinz,' the boy said with some pride.

'Prince, huh?' Lee looked at the tangled and rather dirty puppy with its tongue lolling out of the side of its mouth. 'Well, I suppose he is in your eyes, honey.'

Herr Schneider looked at them in some astonishment when Lee rode into his farmyard with Rudi, having decided that that was the best and nearest place to take him, but the boy broke into a torrent of excited German with much pointing to the dog and to Lee. The farmer looked at the dog and then seemed to be giving Rudi some directions, for he wrote a name and address down for him. Lee had been watching them until Rudi came and looked pleadingly up at her.

'Please, *Fräulein*, you take animal doctor?'

Lee smiled at him reassuringly. 'Of course.' She hoisted him up in the saddle again and followed Herr

Schneider's directions to the vet's house. She was thankful to find that he spoke some English.

'Is not too bad, *Fräulein*. Is not broken,' he told them. 'Keep strapped up for one week, then bring the *Hundchen* back.'

Rudi beamed at him and carefully lifted the bandaged Prinz into his arms, but his face swiftly fell again when the vet named his fee. 'Please,' he looked imploringly at Lee, 'I no money.'

'Well, I have enough, so we don't have to worry, do we?'

Once outside Lee turned to look at the boy. 'I think I had better take you home now. Where do you live?'

'*Bitte?*' Rudi looked at her uncertainly.

'Home? Where is it?'

His face cleared and he gave his gap-toothed and thoroughly engaging grin. '*Ist* Schloss Reistoven.'

For a bewildered moment Lee could only stare at him, then, looking at Rudi's faded shirt and patched leather trousers, realised that there was probably a small army of servants at the Schloss and that Rudi must be the son of one of them.

'Good, I'm going that way myself,' she smiled. The boy obviously hadn't understood, but her smile was all the assurance he needed. Two minutes later they were all three once more sitting on the poor horse's back, but this time, instead of taking the fork in the track leading to her own house, Lee took the left fork that led to the Schloss Reistoven; to the lair of the king of the castle, she thought wryly, and sincerely hoped that she wouldn't encounter him on the way.

The track led to the back of the castle, to a large old gate that stood wide open and was obviously a sort of tradesmen's entrance, if a castle could be described as having such a thing. A wide, tarmac road started from this gate and ran round the outside of the high stone ramparts of a medieval curtain wall towards what Lee guessed must be the gatehouse of the castle, and then on down the steep hillside to the village. Looking through the open gateway, she could see a cobbled way leading to a large stable area and vast coachhouses, all well maintained and clean as a new pin. Not wanting to linger longer than necessary, she dismounted and took Prinz from Rudi while he scrambled to the ground.

'Goodbye, Rudi,' she smiled at him. 'Take care of Prinz.'

But the boy caught her hand before she could climb back into the saddle. 'Please, where you go?'

'To my house. To the Chalet Alpenrose,' she told him.

He nodded his tousled head and, clutching the puppy tightly, turned to run through the gateway, disappearing into a small doorway at the foot of one of the towers.

Rather tiredly, Lee got back on the horse and set off to return down the track. At the brow of the hill she turned to look back at the Schloss Reistoven, a jumble of turrets and gables and mellow, red-brown roofs that reflected the sunlight, as they had done for hundreds of years. How could she even hope to fight the owner of all that? Someone who had the strength and power of generations of overlords behind him, an autocratic man of indomitable purpose who viewed her feeble efforts to thwart him with the contempt they probably deserved. For the first time feeling depressed at the enormity of what she had undertaken, she slowly rode back to another night alone in the chalet.

Deciding that work was the antidote to her fit of the blues, she spent the whole of the next day on cleaning out the other first floor rooms and sandpapering the woodwork ready for painting.

'*Fräulein!* Fräulein Summers!' a shrill voice interrupted her as she applied a first coat of primer paint to the bedroom window frames. Poking her head through the window, she saw Rudi standing outside the house with Prinz beside him, securely tied by a piece of twine. She beckoned him up and he ran up the stairs to greet her, jabbering away in German.

'Hey, wait a minute!' Lee laughed at him. 'I don' understand. *Nicht's versteh'n.*

Excitedly he began to run through the rooms and Lee only just saved the tin of paint from going flying beneath Prinz's paws.

'But you're so clean! I almost didn't recognise you.' She grinned at the well-scrubbed, slick-haired little boy in his spotless shirt and pressed trousers.

'It has been a great effort to keep him smart until we got here, and I'm quite sure that in five minutes he will be dirty again.'

The voice came from behind Lee and she spun round to see a woman hesitating in the doorway.

'May I come in too?'

'Why, yes, of course.'

As the stranger stepped into the room Lee recognised the middle-aged woman she had seen with Max at the village church. She was wearing a simple but well-cut dress of pale blue to match her eyes, her slightly greying fair hair drawn back in a French pleat. She was slim and elegant as only a European woman knows how to be and made Lee feel gauche in her jeans and crumpled shirt. But the elder woman's smile was friendly as she came forward to shake hands.

'*Guten Tag*, Fräulein Summers. I am Anna von Reistoven, Rudi's grandmother. He has told me how bravely you climbed down to rescue him. I'm afraid he is always getting into mischief, that one, but we are most grateful to you that he is here with us.'

Lee found herself flushing under her warm smile. 'But it was nothing,' she protested hurriedly. 'He was only about eight feet down. He probably exaggerated when he told you the story.'

But Frau von Reistoven insisted on thanking her again and then asked her how she liked Austria. Soon they were chatting easily enough, although Lee couldn't get it out of her mind that this fashionably dressed woman must be Max's mother. Which made Rudi Max's son, she supposed, although he didn't look a bit like him, for Rudi was as dark as Max was fair. Perhaps Max's wife was dark-haired.

Up to then their conversation had been on general topics, but now Frau von Reistoven said, 'I must admit, *Fräulein*, that I have been curious to make your acquaintance ever since Max first told me of your arrival here.' Her English was very good but not as fluent as Max's, and her accent was slightly heavier.

Lee looked at her with some misgivings. Was this another von Reistoven she would have to fight? 'He told you about me?'

'Oh, yes. I haven't seen him so—put out—is that the correct phrase? for quite some time. He thought that he had finished with all the trouble over the Alpenrose estate at last.'

'I suppose you think that I ought to have sold to him, that I'm mad not to?' Lee said wryly.

Frau von Reistoven smiled. 'On the contrary. I think you have done exactly the right thing,' she said surprisingly.

Lee stared. 'You do?'

'But certainly. I think you should hold out against him as long as you can. He will win in the end, of course,' she added with a smile. 'He always does, he is that kind of man. But at least you will have taught him that he can't take matters for granted where a determined woman is concerned, and that is a very good thing. I'm entirely on your side,' she said approvingly.

With a delighted smile, Lee said impulsively, 'You're not a bit like Max.'

The other woman raised her eyebrows. 'I should hope not, indeed! Max has had his own way for far too long, it is time that someone taught him a lesson.' Then she noticed Lee's sleeping bag in the recess and her cooking stove in the fireplace. 'But, *Fräulein*, you are not living here at the chalet?'

'Well, yes, I am,' Lee admitted. 'I'm doing all the decorating myself, you see, and it's much more convenient to live on the premises rather than commute from the hotel.'

'But don't you find it rather—er—primitive?' Frau von Reistoven asked delicately.

'Yes, it is a bit, especially when the workmen are here. But I hope that they will have finished in a few more days.'

Frau von Reistoven looked at her consideringly for a few seconds but then turned away to look round the room. 'I remember this house when my cousin Erika lived here. She was your great-aunt, you know. Did you ever meet her?'

'No. No, I didn't.'

'That was a shame. She would have liked you, I think.' Frau von Reistoven paused as if she had suddenly thought of something. 'I have just realised that that makes you a relation of mine.'

'An extremely remote one,' Lee laughed.

'But a relation, nevertheless. And I cannot allow any of my relations to live in conditions such as these when there are lots of rooms, and bathrooms,' she added as she noted Lee's plastic washing bowl, 'just standing empty at the Schloss.'

Lee looked at her silently, no longer smiling.

Coming across to her, Frau von Reistoven put her hands on Lee's shoulders and looked at her steadily. 'Yes, my child, I know you are thinking that I left your great-uncle to live here in these conditions. But will you believe me when I tell you that I came here and I tried, not once but several times, to persuade him to come and make his home with us at the Schloss? But he was an extremely determined old man and he had taken it into his head that Max was his enemy, so there was nothing I could do or say that would move him. It made me very sad, *Fräulein*, especially when he would not accept any help from me.' She paused, then smiled mischievously. 'I do hope you aren't going to be quite so—determined?'

With a little chuckle, Lee said, 'You put it far more gently than Max does.' Then more seriously went on 'It's very kind of you to invite me, Frau von Reistoven but ...'

'But you are not going to accept?'

'No.' Lee shook her head. 'I think it's better that I stay here.'

'Oh, dear, did that big son of mine frighten you so much?' Frau von Reistoven asked in dismay.

Smiling slightly, Lee said, 'No, it's not that. It's just that I ...' She broke off looking rather pleadingly at her.

The older woman nodded. 'Very well, *Fräulein*, I won't press you any more. I understand how you feel.'

'Please, won't you call me Lee?'

'Thank you, my dear, and may Rudi and I call and visit you again?'

'Of course.'

Soon they took their leave and as Lee waved to them from the balcony her feelings were very mixed indeed. Max's mother seemed so genuine and kind, she just didn't seem to be the sort of person who would stand by and let Max do what he had done to her great-uncle. Lee watched them for a long time before she sighed and turned back to her work.

By the time she had finished her fingertips felt raw and her arms ached from painting, so she was more than pleased when Herr Kreuz's car bumped along the track to the house and drew up outside. He had brought old Herr Staffler with him and both men were loud in their praise of all the work she had done, which made Lee feel much better. Herr Kreuz told her that he had arranged for an application to have water and drainage laid on at the chalet.

'But I can't afford that,' Lee said in some dismay. 'You know I only have enough money to pay for the repairs.'

'Yes, yes,' the solicitor hastened to reassure her. 'But if you have planning permission for them it will be a big selling point in your favour.'

'Oh, I see. How do I have to go about getting it?'

'You have to go to Bergheim, to the Länder office— that is the State office,' he explained, 'and fill in an application form. I have to go to Bergheim myself the day after tomorrow and, if you are free, I could take you and help you to fill in the necessary forms. But unfortunately I cannot bring you back as I have to go on to visit a client.'

Lee thanked him warmly and the solicitor then added to his kindness by inviting her back to his house for supper, an invitation Lee was only too pleased to accept as she was already missing the meals she had taken for granted at the hotel. Herr Staffler had also been invited, but after one or two glasses of wine the old man's sole topic of conversation became almost a tirade of abuse against the von Reistovens and all that they stood for. Herr Kreuz tried several times to change the subject, but always the old man brought it back to his hatred for Max and the wrongs he had done Howard Canning. Lee had to sit there and listen, but she wondered uncomfortably if her great-uncle, too, had been as vindictive and unreasonable as Herr Staffler.

Both Lee and Herr Kreuz stood staring in dismay at the official in the Länder office at Bergheim. Apologetically he said, 'I'm sorry, *Fräulein*, but there is nothing I can do. Herr von Reistoven has already told us that in no circumstances will he allow water and drainage pipes to be laid across his land. And as your property is completely surrounded by the von Reistoven estates . . .' He shrugged eloquently.

Dispiritedly they left the office. The solicitor tried to cheer Lee up by saying that he would try to find some way round it, but she knew that it was a forlorn hope He hurried off to keep his appointment, leaving Lee to walk angrily to the bus-station. A sense of helpless frustration gripped her as she experienced the first taste of Max's ability to thwart her plans. He had only to issue an order and there was nothing she could do about it. In this area he was all-powerful and to try to fight him would be like trying to batter down the stone walls of the Schloss with her bare hands.

As Lee walked back towards the town centre she noticed that the sky had clouded over and that there was the cold chill of an approaching storm in the air. She was wearing a pale pink sun-dress that was a perfect foil to her tanned skin and dark hair, but now that the sun had gone in her bare arms began to feel chilly. Quickly she hurried along, her thoughts filled with bitterness as she realised how easily Max could stop her if he wanted to. It's a wonder he let me get this far, she thought resentfully; then it suddenly occurred to her that the work *had* come to a standstill, for the workmen hadn't yet returned from their emergency job. Lee caught her breath; had Max engineered that, too? She certainly wouldn't put it past him!

Turning into the market square, she continued to hurry along, but came to an abrupt halt as she recognised a tall figure on the other side of the street. Her thoughts had been so full of Max that she blinked in surprise, but there was no mistaking him as he walked briskly towards his car which was parked further along. Without hesitation Lee plunged across the road after him, to be noisily blared at by a driver who had to apply his brakes sharply to avoid hitting her. She hardly spared him a glance but dashed on down the street determined to catch up with Max.

At last her running feet brought her up behind him and she put out a hand to pluck at his sleeve and swing him round to face her. She was panting a little from her run, her chest heaving and the glow of exertion in her face. Her eyes were glowing, too, but with good old-fashioned rage. 'Just a minute. I want a word with you!'

Max's look of surprise on seeing her rapidly changed to one of exasperation. 'On the contrary, Fräulein Summers, I'm quite sure that no further words are necessary between us. On several occasions I have given you good advice which you consistently refuse to listen to. Apart from telling you that you are the most stubborn, self-willed woman I have ever met, I really have nothing more to say,' he finished crushingly.

Lee looked up at him, her hand still restrainingly on his sleeve. 'Oh, but I think you do. I think you have a great deal to say. I've just been to the Landesbüro,' she said deliberately.

His mouth tightened, but before he could answer there was a sudden violent crack of thunder and the heavens opened to let fall a torrential burst of rain;

rain that came pelting down in huge drops that smacked and hissed on the still warm pavements.

'This way,' Max took off his jacket and held it over her head as they ran along the road towards the Mercedes. He had the passenger door open in a trice and bundled her in before hurrying round to the other side, but already the material at the front of her sun-dress was soaked through.

A lock of hair clung damply to Max's forehead as he climbed in beside her and shut the door against the downpour.

'Have you ever been in the mountains during a storm?'

When Lee shook her head he started up the car and drove out of the town, the windscreen wipers working furiously to give a clear field of vision. About a mile outside Bergheim, Max drew up on one of the flattened-out parking places on the side of a mountain, constructed so that tourists could take photographs and admire the view. But there was nothing to admire now; there was instead the unforgettable experience of hearing the thunder magnified a hundred times as each clap reverberated against the mountains and echoed dizzily back again. The jagged flashes of lightning lit up the entire range, breaking apart the thick black clouds that hid them and playing hide-and-seek among the peaks. It was a great cacophony of sound and light that hurt the ears and dulled the senses, it was heart-stopping in its intense primeval power and magnificence.

Almost as suddenly as it had begun the lightning eased and the thunder rumbled wearily away across the valley like a tired old man who had outgrown his strength. The rain, too, had stopped, and they sat together in awed silence for some time before Lee turned to this man of the mountains and said bluntly, 'Why won't you let me have water and drainage laid on at the châlet?'

Max turned his head and looked at her, his expression unreadable. 'Do you really have to ask that question?'

Lee stared back at him in mounting anger. 'No, I don't suppose I do,' she said caustically. 'You want that land and you intend to make sure that no one else gets it. I worked for two years in a solicitor's office and in that time I learned a lot about mean, underhand people, but believe me, Herr von Reistoven, you take the prize! I'm only just starting to really understand why Uncle Howard hated you so much, but now I see that you're the worst kind of despot—one who wants everything for himself and can't stand to let others have what is rightfully theirs. You sit up there in your eyrie and manipulate others' lives, wielding the power you have to slowly grind people down until they ...'

Her words were choked off abruptly as Max released his grip on the steering wheel and swung towards her. He caught her by one shoulder, but his other hand went to her throat, effectively silencing her. His eyes were murderous and Lee suddenly knew fear, real, mind-bending fear, and adding to the terror came the knowledge that no one knew she was here with this man, alone on the mountainside where one push could send her headlong to her death.

He must have read it in her eyes, but he didn't release her, just stroked her neck slowly with his thumb while he continued to look at her.

'Is this what I have to do to get through to you? Frighten you into listening to me?' His face was very close to hers. Lee tried to turn her head away, but he forced it back with ease, the look in his eyes different now.

Then, amazingly, he let her go and sat back in his

seat. 'Cigarette?' He seemed completely in control of himself again.

'N-no.'

He lit one himself and opened the window to let the smoke out. The clouds had almost disappeared now and the watery sun had started to warm the earth again.

'My mother tells me that you're camping in the chalet?'

'Yes.' Lee still felt completely unnerved.

'Was it because of me that you refused her hospitality?'

'Not completely. It just didn't seem right to . . .'

'To fraternise with the enemy?' he finished for her drily. 'You may not believe this, Fräulein Summers, but I'm far from being your enemy. If you listen to old Herr Staffler and Herr Kreuz they'll talk you into doing far more to the chalet and spending far more money on it than you intended. And they won't be doing it to help you, only to spite me through you.' He looked at her shrewdly. 'It was their idea to apply for water and drainage, wasn't it? Not yours?'

Lee bit her lip. 'They're only trying to help me when I'm in a strange country. And Uncle Howard trusted them, so why shouldn't I?'

Rather tiredly Max said, 'The mood you're in, you wouldn't believe me if I told you. But this you can believe: if I can stop them from using you by blocking your plans, than I shan't hesitate to do so. Until you come to your senses, that is,' he added crushingly.

'I suppose that's why you took the workmen away?' said Lee, anger still in her voice.

'What do you mean?'

'Isn't it a bit late to start acting the innocent?' she asked bitingly. 'You know very well that the workmen left four days ago to go to what they called a two-day job and they haven't come back, and I don't suppose they ever will, not now I know just where I stand with you!'

Tersely Max said, 'I had nothing to do with that.'

'No?' Lee said insultingly, then turned to stare out of the window. 'If you don't mind, I'd like to go back to Bergheim now. I have to catch the bus.'

He continued to look at her averted profile for a moment, then, without a word, reversed the car and drove back the way they had come, but he didn't stop in Bergheim, instead he drove her silently back to Ausbach to where the track to the chalet branched off the road.

'I'm afraid you'll have to walk from here,' he said coldly. 'I don't feel like risking the car up that track.'

Her voice heavy with sarcasm, Lee answered, 'I hardly expected anything else. After all, you made my great-uncle walk across these fields in all weathers, didn't you? What a pity I'm not as old as he was. You'd get far more of a kick out of it then, wouldn't you?'

She went to get out of the car, but with a swift movement Max pinned her back against the seat with his arm.

Grimly he said, 'Look around you. This valley is surrounded by steep mountains. Your uncle drove an extremely noisy old car. He insisted on driving it even in the middle of winter when everywhere was thick with snow. One loud noise could start an avalanche that might destroy a dozen farms and houses; a loud noise like the broken exhaust of a car.' Max's eyes were like slate as he added scornfully, 'Now get out of my car, child, and go and play with your doll's house.'

White-faced, Lee got out of the Mercedes and started up the track. When she heard the car pull away and knew that it was out of sight she started running and didn't stop until she was safely inside the house, the door firmly shut behind her.

The heavy rain during the storm had found its way under the tarpaulin over the hole in the roof and she was able to work out the anger she felt while mopping up the puddles that had collected on the top floor of the chalet. After she had fastened the cover more securely she went to make herself a meal, but then remembered that she had run out of fuel for the cooker. She had intended to buy some more in Ausbach on the way home, but Max giving her a lift had put all thoughts of it out of her head, so she had to make do with bread, cheese and an apple. Outside the sky had clouded over again and she fervently hoped that there wouldn't be another storm.

Taking out her writing pad, she tried to write to Richard. Since moving into the chalet she had been so busy that she hadn't had time to answer his last letter, but now she found it difficult to know what to write. In her previous letter she had explained why she felt she couldn't sell to Max, but Richard had completely failed to understand. He wanted her to come home at once, promised to go out to Austria himself as soon as he was free and sort things out. Instinctively Lee knew that 'sorting things out' to Richard would mean immediately selling to Max, probably with profuse apologies for her own behaviour. After only a couple of paragraphs she pushed the letter aside; she was putting down only commonplace phrases; better to wait until tomorrow when she was fresh.

It must have been about one o'clock in the morning when the thunderclap startled Lee into quivering wakefulness. It had been very loud, very close overhead. Lightning flashes came through the uncurtained windows to make the room momentarily as light as day and she shrank back into her sleeping bag, glad of the solid walls of the recess all round her. Rain pelted on to the tarpaulin and then she heard it flapping loudly in the wind. The darned thing must have come loose again! Reluctantly she crawled out of the recess and lit the lamp, knowing that if she didn't fix it the floor above would soon be sodden. Once up the narrow staircase she set the lamp down on the windowsill, then climbed up on an old chair to try to reach the loose corner of the tarpaulin. The wind, however, had other ideas and constantly blew it away from her outstretched hands. Exasperated, Lee stood on tiptoe and made a grab for it. For a second she thought she had it and gave a small cry of triumph, but then the rickety chair tipped under her and she found herself crashing heavily to the ground!

Slowly, dazedly, she tried to sit up, but let out a sharp cry of pain when she went to put her weight on her right wrist. The room started to spin crazily and she had to lean against the wall until it stilled enough for her to open her eyes. Feeling slightly sick, she managed to get to her feet. Apart from her wrist she seemed to have escaped unharmed, but it hurt like hell and she was afraid it might be broken. Picking up the lamp in her left hand, she gingerly made her way downstairs again. Experimentally she tried her fingers and was immensely relieved when she found that she could move them. Lee's sole first-aid experience was restricted to what she had learnt as a Girl Guide, but she seemed to remember that sprains should be soaked in cold water. When she had decided to live at the chalet she had bought a two-gallon polythene water container, but as soon as she picked this up she realised that she had used the last of the water to wash in last night. Damn! Now she would have to go out into the storm to fill the container at the stream.

It was a ridiculously difficult task to pull her mackintosh on over her nightdress, but at last she was ready. Going back into the kitchen, she picked up the water-container and turned towards the door just as a bright flash of lightning lit the room. Lee stopped dead in her tracks, a little whimper of terror escaping from her throat. The lightning had outlined the figure of a man just passing the window! She stood frozen, unable to move for what seemed like light years, then a loud knock sounded on the wooden door.

Lee tried to speak, but could only make a strangled noise. The knocking came again and then the door was pushed open. Max stood in the doorway, rain dripping from his trench-coat and plastering his hair to his forehead, the thunder loud behind him. Lee stared at him with wide, terrified eyes. Quickly he came in and shut the door just as she felt her knees starting to buckle beneath her.

'You—you scared me half to death,' she faltered.

'Here, drink some of this.' He took one look at her white face and held out a hip flask of brandy.

'Thank you.' Lee took the flask with trembling fingers, but then realised that she couldn't unscrew the top. 'C-could you undo it for me, please? I've hurt my hand.'

'Let me look,' he commanded. He took her small hand in his big ones and gently began to explore her wrist. Already it was beginning to swell alarmingly. 'It doesn't feel broken, but you must have sprained it badly. You'll need to have it X-rayed to make sure, of course.' He poured some of the brandy into a plastic cup and gave it to her.

Lee sipped it gratefully, the spirit warming and reviving her. Glancing up, she saw Max looking down at her with an expression half exasperated, half rueful. The flashes of light in the dimly lit room highlighted the planes of his face and gave him an oddly satanic appearance. When he saw her looking at him his expression changed wholly to exasperation.

'What were you doing to hurt your arm at this time of night?'

'The tarpaulin over the roof came loose and I was trying to fix it, but the chair overturned. I must have fallen with my wrist under me. I was going out to get some water to bathe it when you arrived.'

'I'll get it for you.' He picked up the container and turned towards the door.

'But you'll get soaked,' Lee felt she had to protest.

Max grinned crookedly. 'No more than I am already.'

Within five minutes he was back. 'You'll have to take off that mac,' he remarked as he poured water into a bowl. He hung up his own raincoat and then helped Lee to take off hers. She felt strangely vulnerable with only her thin nightdress on, but Max was completely impersonal, although infinitely gentle, as he helped her to bathe her wrist.

'While you're soaking that I'd better go and see if there's anything I can do with the tarpaulin.'

When he came back Lee said, 'You haven't told me yet why you came?'

'I saw a light in the upper part of the chalet and thought you might be in trouble.'

Lee flushed, remembering how angrily they had parted earlier in the day. 'It was kind of you to come yourself. But you could have sent someone else, surely·'

'I could,' Max replied evenly. He lifted her hand from the bowl and carefully began to pat it dry with a towel. 'But I was the one who saw your light, so why turn someone else out of bed? That looks less puffy now, I think. Have you a scarf or something we can make into a sling?'

'There's one in my smaller suitcase in the bedroom,' Lee told him.

Expertly he made a sling and went behind her to tie

it, his fingers warm against her neck. 'That will have to suffice until it's X-rayed, I'm afraid.' He picked up her mac and held it for her to put her left arm in. 'Here, put this back on and we'll get going.'

'Going? Where?' For a moment Lee thought he was going to drive her to a hospital straightaway.

'Back to the Schloss, of course.' Then he saw the expression on her face and his mouth hardened. 'Look, you can argue all you want, but I'm not leaving you alone here unable to look after yourself. So you can either come with me willingly or I'll pick you up and carry you,' he said forcefully.

'That doesn't give me a great deal of choice, does it?' Lee said unsteadily.

Max sighed and ran his hand through his hair. 'I'm sorry, I didn't mean to bully you, but I can't leave you here. You must see that,' he reasoned.

'All right, I'll come with you,' Lee agreed, suddenly feeling very tired.

'I'll get your cases.'

'It's really very kind of you,' she said stiffly when he came back.

'Not at all, that's what neighbours are for.' There was a sardonic look in his blue eyes that made Lee drop her own.

Carefully turning out the lamp, Max led the way outside. He locked the door and then helped her down the stairs to the ground, using his large frame to shelter her from the worst of the rain, but the storm was dying away now, its full force spent. He had driven over in a Land-rover and they were soon inside and driving over the track towards the Schloss. Lee looked back at the Chalet Alpenrose, looking dark and empty behind her, and felt a sharp stab of despair; would it ever be repaired?

Max must have seen her look, for he said quietly,

'Coming to stay at the Schloss Reistoven doesn't mean that you've lost the battle, Lee.'

He had used her christian name for the first time and somehow its use seemed to create an intimacy between them in the metal confines of the Land-rover.

'No? What does it mean, then? You've driven the workmen away and now I won't be able to do any work myself until my wrist heals,' she said dispiritedly

Pulling up inside the cobbled stableyard of the Schloss, Max switched off the engine and turned to face her. 'Your arm must be paining you a great deal. I'm sure that nothing else would make you feel so defeated. Which is a great shame, because I was just beginning to enjoy our fight,' he commented outrageously.

'Enjoy it!' Lee stared at him indignantly. 'Why, you —you big, conceited . . .

Max laughed. 'That's more like what I've come to expect from you.'

Against her will Lee had to laugh rather weakly with him. He helped her out of the car and hurried her across to the tower that she had seen Rudi disappear into the other day. They went up a wide circular staircase and entered a stone-floored corridor with white painted walls on the second floor.

'My mother will be pleased that you've come to the Schloss,' Max remarked. 'She was worried about you.

'That was kind of her.' They had gone through a curtained archway into another corridor running at right angles to the first and Lee stopped to stare. This must be the part of the castle that the von Reistovens used, for now the floor was thickly carpeted, the panelled walls adorned with paintings and the window embrasures furnished with carved chests or beautiful antique chairs and sofas. Rather nervously she said, 'I do hope your wife won't mind me turning up in the middle of the night like this.'

There was some amusement in Max's eyes as he turned back to look at her. 'But I'm not married.'

'Oh.' Lee digested this. 'Rudi isn't your son, then?'

'No, he's my sister's child. He's only staying here while she and her husband are abroad.' He had stopped at a door near the head of a staircase and held it open for her. 'I think you will find this room is ready for you.'

As Lee entered she caught her breath in delight, for the room was dominated by a four-poster bed, not a full-sized one that she would feel lost in, but a smaller version with its heavy tapestries replaced by the flowing softness of white lace with a matching counterpane. The rest of the furniture was also antique but of the light, eighteenth-century French style rather than the heavier medieval period.

Her pleasure showed in her face as she turned back to Max standing so tall in the doorway. 'It's a lovely room. Thank you.'

'There's a bathroom through there,' he told her, indicating a small door set into the wall. He set her cases down and then helped her out of her mac. 'Do you have everything you need?'

'Yes.'

'Then if you're sure you can manage, I'll wish you goodnight.'

'Goodnight.'

But instead of leaving he paused as if about to say something more. His eyes ran over her slender figure outlined through the thin nightdress and Lee instinctively raised her hands to cover herself. Max smiled thinly and went out, quietly shutting the door behind him. After a moment Lee gave a little shrug and went to run her hands lovingly over the deep patina of a small but very beautiful writing desk that stood against one wall. She had always loved antiques and it gave her great pleasure to have them around her in a setting that suited them so perfectly. A sharp throb of pain from her arm made her slip out of her shoes and slide between the fresh, lavender-scented covers of the four-poster. It had been a long, nerve-racking day and she felt incredibly tired, but it was some time before her mind let her sleep.

Max had said that it wasn't a defeat to come to the Schloss, but to Lee it was showing weakness to have given in so easily. She could have stayed at the chalet for the night and then made her own way to a doctor's in the morning. But Max would never have allowed her to do that, she knew. He would have been quite capable of fulfilling his threat and carrying her out of the chalet! Fretfully she wondered why he had been so anxious to get her out. Her mind filled with recollections of legal cases she had come across where locks had been changed on houses while the owners were away and others had claimed possession. Was that what Max intended to do? Would he try to take the Chalet Alpenrose from her while he had her safely out of the way at the Schloss? The pain in her wrist made her toss and turn uncomfortably, her mind was full of doubts and she was beginning to heartily wish that she had never even heard of the Chalet Alpenrose!

CHAPTER FIVE

RAYS of sunlight filtered through the latticed windows when Lee woke the next morning and it took her a few moments before she realised where she was, before she remembered that she had breached the mighty bastions of the Schloss Reistoven. Slipping out of bed, she crossed the thick carpet to look out of the pair of tall, arched windows that lit the room. They opened on to the west side of the castle grounds giving an impressive view of a traditional European parterre garden with little paths dissecting symmetrical flower beds to form intricate patterns broken only by an occasional statue or stone seat. Behind this cultured neatness and divided by a high hedge, Lee could see the serried ranks of fruit trees in an orchard, and to the right of that the old walls of a kitchen garden. Over to the left, though, beyond the curtain wall the ground dropped abruptly in a series of steep steps to a wooded and verdant valley half veiled by the morning mists. All traces of yesterday's storm had disappeared and there was the promise of a hot, fine day.

Lee turned as a maid knocked and entered. She indicated Lee's luggage. 'Shall I unpack for you, *Fräulein*?' While she was doing this Lee opened the door in the wall and found it led to a small but beautifully fitted out bathroom. The maid waited for her to finish dressing, then led her down a bewildering number of flights of stairs and along several corridors before arriving at a room that the girl told her was the breakfast room.

Here Frau von Reistoven immediately rose to greet her. 'My dear child, I was so sorry to hear of your accident. Is your wrist very painful?'

Lee assured her that it was much better, but Frau von Reistoven told her that she had made an appointment to take her to the local hospital for an X-ray.

'Max would have taken you himself,' she explained, 'but he had to go out unexpectedly on business and won't be back until this evening.'

Grimly Lee wondered just what important business had called Max away so urgently, but was given no time to dwell on the subject as Frau von Reistoven con-

tinued to chat to her while offering her round hot rolls
-*Semmerl*, she called them—that were hard on the
outside but soft and delicious when you broke them
open. These she spread for her with sweet butter and
home-made jam, and there was rich, creamy coffee to
drink. Lee suddenly realised how hungry she was and
ate appreciatively while Frau von Reistoven watched
her in some amusement.

After breakfast they were taken in a chauffeur-driven
car to the hospital, where the X-ray showed that there
were no bones broken. A doctor put an elastic bandage
on Lee's wrist and told her that she would be able
to use it normally in a week or so. On their return
journey Lee had hoped to catch a glimpse of the chalet,
but the driver took the main road up the steep hill to
the huge stone gatehouse of the Schloss. He honked the
horn and the massive gates were immediately opened
by an elderly man who touched his hat as they went
through. There was a steep cobbled way giving Lee
only a short time to glimpse the jumble of turrets and
gables before they came to a covered bridge over a
moat, long ago filled in, and then on through another
gateway and a short dark tunnel to finally emerge into
a large, sunny courtyard.

The chauffeur opened the door for her as she stepped from the car and she gazed round her with delight.
This part of the castle was built in the form of an open
square enclosing an inner court. If Lee could have
imagined it at all she would have expected the courtyard to have been a grey, shadowed place, but instead
it had been lovingly transformed into a garden with
rich velvet lawns, shrubberies and flower beds that
were glowing jewels against the rough grey stone of the
walls. Fountains played in the centre and climbing
plants, dripping with flowers, encircled the ancient
arched windows. It was a magical place and all the

more lovely for being unexpected.

Lee turned reluctantly to follow Frau von Reistoven, who led her across the courtyard to a great doorway which had a heavy stone lintel with a bas-relief in the shape of a shield bearing a coat of arms. The door was of oak and very old, held together by iron bands and studded with bolts, while the handle was a bronze lion's head with a large ring in its mouth which had to be turned before the door would open. They crossed a richly furnished vestibule and entered a panelled corridor decorated with carved chests, tapestries and armour, all of such high quality that Lee was lost in wonder and had come to the door the chauffeur was holding open for them before she realised it. The room was definitely a female room with light, pretty furniture and a suite of comfortable armchairs.

'This is my sitting-room,' Frau von Reistoven told her. 'Would you like to rest before lunch or would you prefer a stroll round the grounds?'

Lee opted for the grounds, which turned out to be Frau von Reistoven's particular interest and of which she was justly proud, although Lee found the number of different gardens round the Schloss somewhat bewildering in their variety.

'Good heavens, I had no idea that gardening could be so complex,' she said admiringly as they came upon a water garden fashioned from one of the streams that flowed down from the heights above.

Frau von Reistoven laughed. 'I'm afraid I spend too much time on it, but it has been my favourite hobby since I was a child. Max indulges me but he prefers to cultivate the timber forests, farms and vineyards.'

'Vineyards? You have those, too? I haven't seen any round here.'

'No, the vines do not grow in this area, but we have several in the *Länder* of Lower Austria for example, in the Wachau region, which is quite near Vienna. It is beautiful there. Perhaps you may see it before you go.'

They had circled the castle and now came to a terrace with the very modern addition of a kidney-shaped swimming pool. Frau von Reistoven smiled at Lee's surprised face and said, 'This is Max's toy. He likes to keep fit and swims before breakfast every morning. Please use it whenever you wish.'

Lee thanked her warmly, making a mental note to swim only in the afternoon or evening so as not to clash with the king of the castle!

Later that evening the maid, Trudi, a village girl of about her own age, directed Lee along the corridor leading to the great hall and told her that the drawing-room door led off of it. Not quite knowing just how grand dinner in a Schloss was likely to be, Lee had chosen a dull red, full-skirted dress that enriched her dark colouring to perfection, its deep-cut neckline displaying a provocative hint of her firm young breasts. The corridor turned a corner and she found herself on the threshold of the great hall and, in this instance, the adjective was inadequate. It was a vast room, two storeys high and roofed with enormous dark beams. A gallery ran round three sides of the upper storey and from this descended a flight of exquisitely carved stone stairs dimly lit by wall sconces. Along one wall was a row of suits of armour, the light reflecting on the polished surfaces of helmet and breastplate, giving the armoured shapes an illusion of life and movement. Collections of swords, pikes and other weapons were arranged in intricate patterns on the panelled walls above, with here and there the tattered remnants of a once-proud battle banner hanging forlornly in the still air. A huge stone fireplace dominated one corner of the room and here again was displayed the von Reistoven armorial bearings.

The fire was now unlit, for the night was warm, but Lee could imagine how the room would come alive when the hearth was filled with flaming logs. It was a room that seemed to be waiting; waiting again to hear the blowing of war trumpets, to feel the tramp of the knights in their mail and armour as they took up the great battleaxes and two-handed swords and prepared once more to fight.

Lee half shut her eyes and spun gently round, the red dress leaping into shafts of flame as it flared round her. She was lost in the pictures of the past that the hall had evoked; of knights galloping down the lists for the glory of championship, of lovers hastening to their ladies' bowers. She noticed the gallery for the first time and wondered idly if the troubadour, Blondel, had played there on his search for King Richard the Lionheart. Then she stood still abruptly. A man who was much larger than any figment of her imagination, more vital and definitely more real than any wraith, stood at the corner of the gallery silently watching her. Lee looked up at him, her heart-shaped face framed in clouds of smoky-black hair.

Max came slowly down the stairs towards her dressed in an immaculate black evening suit, the stark whiteness of his shirt deepening his tan and the cut of the jacket revealing the full breadth of his muscular shoulders. He came and stood before her, in his eyes a look —perhaps a little of amusement, but also something more—yes, definitely something more. Very formally, he bowed and raised Lee's hand to his lips. His touch was light, yet warm and strong. His eyes were blue as the sky as they looked deep into hers and Lee again experienced that breathless, choking feeling that made her hand start to shake in his.

'*Willkommen.* Welcome to my home, Lee,' he said softly. Turning to indicate the gallery where he had stood to watch her, he said, 'Our positions should have been reversed, shouldn't they? It was Juliet who should have stood on the balcony.'

Smiling rather tremulously, Lee managed to say, 'I admit I was day-dreaming. This magnificent room raises a host of pictures. It's the very quintessence of Romance with a capital R, isn't it?'

'To a stranger it must be so, but I have lived here most of my life and I suppose I've become blasé about it. I must try to see it through your eyes,' he said indulgently, rather as if he were speaking to a silly, romantic teenager.

He led her to an archway concealed under the stairs and opened the door into a brilliantly lit and richly furnished drawing-room. There were several people already in the room, but Frau von Reistoven came quickly forward to greet her warmly and to hold her arm while she introduced her to the other guests. Nearly everyone spoke English, one of the men having lived in England for some time, so Lee was quite pleased to find herself placed next to him at dinner.

The meal was a formal one of several courses, but Lee hardly noticed what was served and merely toyed with the food on her plate. She talked and laughed with the people near her, but her eyes kept straying up the long, candlelit table to where Max sat at its head, courteously turning to some remark of the lady on his right, or listening to some long story from the woman on his left; very much the host, very much at ease. It was even more difficult, now, in these surroundings, to visualise him as the man who had been so cruel to her great-uncle.

Once she had turned away from his end of the table to answer a question about London from her neighbour, when she felt that she was being watched. Quickly she turned and found Max looking at her intently. Lee raised her eyes to his and for a moment their glances locked, but then Frau von Reistoven rose and it was time for the ladies to withdraw in the old-fashioned tradition that was still maintained in the Schloss Reistoven.

The rest of the evening passed in a whirl and was over all too quickly. When the others had left Max excused himself and his mother walked Lee to her room and said goodnight, but Lee had never felt less like sleep in all her life. She took out her writing pad and tried to finish her letter to Richard but found writing difficult with her sprained wrist, and anyway, she just couldn't concentrate. Slowly she put down her pen and finally admitted to herself what her emotions had known all along; that she was beginning to be physically attracted to Max! That she was fully aware of him as a man. But she was going to marry Richard, wasn't she? She had no right to feel like that about another man, to want him to touch her, to like to be near him, especially one as ruthless and callous as Max von Reistoven. Looking back, she realised that she had been attracted to him from the first and that was why she had so turned against him when she had found out about him. If she hadn't liked him so much it wouldn't have been so hard to take.

So what if she was—infatuated with him? It was a purely physical thing, and completely one-sided at that. Mentally she knew him for what he was and there was no danger of her feelings taking over, of her making a fool of herself by letting him know how she felt. Not that he was likely to be interested even if she did, she thought with cruel irony, for Max had treated her with contemptuous disdain ever since she had started to fight him. Although, once or twice, there had been that curious light in his eyes. He was probably laughing at what a gullible fool I was, Lee told herself angrily. She would just have to leave the Schloss as soon as she could; to get away from Max and go back home to Richard. Moodily she stood up and crossed to look at herself in the mirror. Her face was pale, her eyes dark and troubled. How could she honestly go back to Richard, marry him, live with him as his wife, when all the time her body ached for someone else's touch?

Pushing open the window, she looked out past the blue and white chevron-patterned shutters, across the rising hills to where the moon lit the snow-covered peaks. Why had she never felt like this about Richard, who was so easy to get along with and who always looked at her with admiration and paid her compliments, instead of calling her a fool and getting angrier with her every time he saw her? She sighed and looked down on to the terrace. The moon was reflected on the still waters of the swimming pool; it looked cool and inviting, suddenly Lee longed to plunge into its depths and tire herself out by sheer physical exertion. Well, Frau von Reistoven had said use it any time, hadn't she?

It took hardly a moment to change into her swimsuit and wrap but rather longer to find her way to the terrace. Quickly she slipped off the blue towelling robe and tucked her hair into her bathing cap. She unwrapped the crêpe bandage and then went to the side to dive cleanly into the water. She swam across the pool under the surface, then came up to do several lengths in a fast, steady crawl until turning to float easily on her back, looking at the castle as the turrets and towers were outlined against the moonlight.

The pungent aroma of cigar-smoke drifted across her nostrils and Lee turned and swam to the steps, knowing who was there before she hauled herself out. Max was reclining comfortably in a lounger, smoking a long Havana cigar. Lee pulled off her cap and shook

her hair free before walking slowly towards him. He
rose and held her robe ready for her to slip into. He
smelt of tobacco and woody after-shave, and very, very
masculine.

'Do you always swim at midnight?' He placed the
robe round her and—and did his hands linger on her
shoulders for just a moment?

'I couldn't sleep.'

He pulled another lounger forward for her. 'Cigarette?'

Lee took one from the case he offered and for a
moment she saw his face clearly in the flare of the
lighter flame. Then she looked quickly away; if she
could see him then he could also see her.

'You swim well. How's the wrist?'

'Tons better, thank you. The doctor said I need
only keep the bandage on for about a week, but I can
use it quite well already.'

'You'd better let me put it back on for you.' He took
the bandage and carefully wrapped it round her wrist.
When he had finished he didn't let go of her hand
straightaway but continued to hold it as though satis-
fying himself that it was on correctly.

Lee couldn't trust herself to look at him. 'Thank
you,' she said as calmly as she could. 'I shall be able
to go back to the chalet tomorrow.'

Immediately he let go of her hand and sat back in
his chair. 'I meant to talk to you about that. I took it
on myself to contact the builder who was working on
the chalet. He went back there this morning but found
that part of the chimney stack was dangerously loose
and it won't be safe to continue work on the roof until
it has been repaired, and it definitely won't be safe for
you to go on living there.'

Lee sat bolt upright and stared at him. 'The chimney was perfectly all right before!' Her eyes glittered

angrily as she stood and faced him. 'I wondered why you were so darn anxious to get me out of the chalet. What have you done to it?'

Max looked up at her coldly. 'Just what is that remark supposed to mean?'

Refusing to be intimidated, Lee swept on angrily, 'Do you think I don't know why you wanted me out of the way? You brought me here just so that you could get to the chalet while my back was turned! I wouldn't put it past you to ...'

As angry as she now, Max too got to his feet. 'You little fool! If I'd wanted to do anything to the chalet I could have done it while you were staying at the hotel. But why should I want to damage something that is rightfully mine? How do you know that the chimney was all right before today? Are you sure the builder examined it?'

'Of course.' Lee wasn't sure, but she wasn't going to let him know that.

Max stared at her, breathing hard. 'Lee, if I had wanted the Alpenrose estate that badly I could have taken it back years ago. As it was, your uncle chose to take it to the law-courts so I couldn't touch it, or I would have kept it in good repair myself. Do you think I like to see the place in such a state? A house that has been in my family for generations?' His jaw tightened. 'And believe it or not, I don't play underhand tricks behind people's backs, especially when they happen to be guests in my home!' he finished on a savage note. For a moment he continued to glare at her, then abruptly stubbed out his half-finished cigar before turning to stride away.

He had taken only a few steps, however, before Lee said hurriedly, 'Max.' He stopped and turned round to face her. Slowly now, she went on, 'Th-that was extremely rude of me. I'm sorry.' She found that she couldn't look at him and instead quite unnecessarily retied the belt of her wrap.

Max didn't answer immediately, but then stirred and walked back to stand close in front of her. Still she didn't look up, so he put a long finger under her chin, tilting her head so that she had to look at him as he regarded her somewhat ruefully. 'We do seem to have the unfortunate effect of striking sparks off one another, don't we? It must be something in our make-up.'

Lee gave a ghost of a smile. 'Perhaps it's because we're *both* as stubborn as mules.'

'Have I been such a tyrant, little one?' he asked gently.

Stupidly Lee felt tears pricking at the back of her eyes at his tone and she could only shake her head, unable to reply, angry with herself because a gentle word from him could have this effect on her.

'Suppose we make a pact,' Max suggested. 'While you're staying at the Schloss we'll call a truce to our— private war. An armed truce, if you like,' he added as he saw the swift spark of suspicion in her eyes. 'But neither of us will do anything about the Alpenrose while you're my guest.' He smiled, a slightly crooked smile. 'It might be a good idea if we didn't even talk about it. But if you should change your mind I'd like you to remember that my offer still stands, plus the cost of the repairs already carried out, of course.'

Watching carefully for his reaction, Lee said, 'And if I still refuse to sell to you?'

He shrugged. 'Let's not worry about that at the moment.'

'Will you try and get it back from me in the law-courts?'

'I never took it to court; it was your great-uncle who did that. I thought you would have taken the trouble to find that out for yourself,' he said with a sharp note in his voice. 'And I hardly think you're in a financial position to contemplate fighting me in court, Lee.'

'No? Aren't you forgetting that my boy-friend is a barrister? I can fight you in any court you like and it won't cost me a penny.'

Max stood very still for a second, then his expression became quite unreadable as he said sarcastically, 'Ah, yes, your unofficial fiancé. How convenient. So, we have reached a stalemate. Do we call a truce or not?'

Unhappily Lee saw that they had ended up at one another's throats yet again and realised that his solution was the only sensible one while they were living under the same roof. 'All right,' she agreed reluctantly. 'But only for the time being.'

He looked amused. 'Somehow I don't think you'll ever win the Nobel Peace Prize, but it will do for a start.' Deliberately he changed the subject. 'Has my mother shown you round the Schloss yet?' And when Lee shook her head, he added, 'Then I expect she will want to do that tomorrow morning, but perhaps you would like to come out with me after lunch. There are one or two calls I have to make that might interest you.'

Lee hesitated for only a second. 'Thank you, I think I should like that.'

Frau von Reistoven took Lee on the promised tour of the Schloss the next morning, and although her hostess answered all her eager questions in detail, Lee couldn't help but notice that she didn't have as much interest and enthusiasm for the castle as she had for the gardens. Lee had all the awe of the British for anything craftsman-made and many of the beautiful antiques had been formed by skilful and caring hands as long ago as the fifteenth century. Reverently she ran her hands over a carved chair, black with age, but with every detail still as delicate and vibrant as when it was made so very long ago.

'But come, you have not yet seen the chapel and the apartments upstairs,' her hostess told her as she lingered yet again.

Soon Lee was bewildered by the number of rooms and wasn't entirely sorry when it was time for lunch; such an abundance of magnificence was too much for one morning. Max didn't join them but sent a message that he would meet Lee later. She found him waiting for her in the courtyard with the Mercedes. Rudi came running out to them, Prinz as usual barking at his heels.

'You cannot take the dog,' Max told him sternly, and Rudi immediately burst into an impassioned argument with him in German that ended with the child going sulkily back into the castle.

'Can't he come?' Lee pleaded, seeing his bowed shoulders and unhappy little face.

'No. He has to learn that he can't take Prinz everywhere.' Max was completely unmoved.

He took her on what was more or less a tour of the von Reistoven estate, visiting two farms where he discussed business with his tenants while Lee was shown round by the farmers' wives, although their conversation was somewhat hampered by their not being able to speak each other's language.

'I do wish I spoke German,' Lee remarked as they drove away. 'I'm sure I missed a great deal by not being able to talk to them.'

'Even if you had spoken German you wouldn't have been able to understand them,' Max informed her. threading the way through a maze of twisting lanes. 'As a rule the highland people speak only their own Austrian dialect and this varies from state to state throughout the country, often from village to village, much as in Britain the dialect changes from north to south.'

'Have you spent much time in England?'

'Why, yes, I spent a year there to study the language before I settled down to running the estates.'

'From what I've seen they must keep you pretty busy?'

'Yes, but there are other business interests that often take me away. In fact I have to go to Vienna very soon to take care of some business affairs and also to see how the vine crop is progressing.'

Their next call was at a forester's hut and to reach it they had to leave the car and walk along a rather overgrown ride for about half a mile. Max looked at the rapidly encroaching scrub and bracken with some dissatisfaction.

'Old Johann is supposed to keep the rides clear, but obviously the job is getting too much for him. I will have to replace him with a younger man.'

'What will he do?' Lee asked curiously.

'He has a married daughter who lives in a nearby village. I will try and persuade him to go and live with her.'

When they reached the hut an old, bald-headed man, his lips sunk into his toothless mouth, came to the door and greeted Max warmly. Max took the man by the arm and walked along a path with him out of earshot, but Lee could tell that the old forester didn't like what he was saying. Eventually, though, he reluctantly nodded his head and Max came back to join her.

'Did he agree to go?'

Max grinned. 'After some argument. But he won't go to live with his daughter; he doesn't like his son-in-law, so he's going to come to the Schloss and help in the stables.' He glanced at her. 'Does that surprise you?

I suppose you expected me to turn him out into the street?'

'N-no, of course not,' Lee said hastily, but the thought had crossed her mind.

'There is always a place at the Schloss for any old servant or their families who have nowhere else to go. They have a pension and they are looked after when they are unable to look after themselves. The same goes for anyone who is ill. The von Reistovens take care of their own, Lee.'

If his conducted tour of the estate had been meant to impress her it had certainly succeeded, but it had also had the adverse effect of making her wonder why, when he had so much, should the Alpenrose estate be so important to him, and now his last remark had given her a clue. Compared to the large areas of land over which he held domain, the chalet and its lands didn't amount to one per cent, but it lay like a festering sore amidst the meticulously cared-for lands around it. But surely even that wouldn't have driven him to the lengths he had taken? Lee thought in bewilderment. She could only presume that Herr Staffler had been right; that Max would never allow any land that had once been part of the estate to pass to outside hands.

Frau von Reistoven was waiting for them in some agitation when they got back to the Schloss. 'Rudi has been away all afternoon,' she told them. 'At first I thought he was sulking because you didn't take him with you, but he didn't come home for tea. Please go out and help look for him, Max.'

Lee insisted on going with him and they set off at once to search the surrounding woodland. They were beginning to feel really worried when at last they heard Prinz barking in the distance.

'I think it came from that direction,' Lee pointed towards a clump of thick scrub and undergrowth hiding the trunks of the taller trees growing among it.

Max pushed the branches aside and they found Prinz crouching at the foot of a tall pine, his pink tongue lolling out of the side of his mouth. 'But where is ...?' There was a shout from above them and there, perched high in the fork of a tree, was Rudi, well and truly stuck. Muttering under his breath, Max climbed carefully up the trunk, holding on to the outsprung branches as he went.

Soon Rudi was back on the ground and hugging Prinz to him. 'He no leave me,' he said happily. 'He stay and guard me.'

Max jumped down beside him and brushed his hands clean. Speaking in German, he said to Rudi, 'That dog is a pest. I expect he led you here?'

'Yes, he chased a squirrel up the tree and I climbed up to catch it, but I couldn't get down.'

There were no other guests for dinner that night, so they ate in what Frau von Reistoven called the small dining-room, which turned out to be a large room in the west wing, admittedly not as large as the main dining-room, but still big enough to easily seat a dozen people without being overcrowded.

Frau von Reistoven smiled as Lee sat down. 'This is so much nicer, don't you think? Max and I always use this room when we are *en famille*.'

Recognising the compliment, Lee responded to it warmly, but a glance at Max revealed a face that plainly disagreed with his mother, even if he was too well-mannered to say so. His mother contributed most of the conversation during dinner and from art in general the topic changed to music and opera and she asked, 'Have you ever seen one of Wagner's operas, Lee? I believe you have a very good opera company in London?'

'Yes, it's one of the finest outside Italy, but unfortu-

nately I've never seen any of Wagner's works. I've heard
the music, of course, but I would love to see one of his
operas performed live.'

Their talk went on to other subjects and Lee had
almost forgotten it altogether when, later that evening,
Max rejoined them after leaving to go to his study for
a short time.

'I've been on the telephone to the opera house at
Bregenz,' he remarked as he poured himself a brandy.
'It seems that *Götterdämmerung* is being performed at
the Music Festival there, so I've booked tickets for us
for tomorrow night.'

Frau von Reistoven clapped her hands in pleasure.
'Why, Max, that's *wunderbar*! To see Wagner for the
first time at Bregenz will be an experience that Lee will
never forget.' She turned to Lee and began, 'You see,
my dear, the opera house is actually . . .'

But Max interrupted her swiftly, 'No, Mother, don't
tell Lee about it yet. I think we should keep it as a
surprise.'

'But of course,' his mother smiled, then added, 'But,
Max, we will have to stay overnight and the hotels will
be full at this time of the year.'

'That, too, is taken care of.' He looked at Lee quizzically. 'But Lee doesn't say anything?'

She looked at him as he stood so tall and straight near
the high mantelshelf. She felt her heart start to hammer
and found it difficult to speak coherently. 'Th-thank
you,' she managed. 'It was very thoughtful of you.'

Perhaps he was disappointed by her lack of enthusiasm, for he merely bowed politely and said, 'It is my
pleasure to please our guest.'

Frau von Reistoven had been right; a visit to the
opera house at Bregenz was definitely an experience
she would never forget. They had set out in the early
afternoon and had driven through the sunny country-

side of the Tyrol to arrive at their hotel near Lake
Constance in time to change for an early dinner. After-
wards they had driven to what appeared to be the entrance to a large building, but when they got inside Lee
had stood stock still in amazement, for the opera house
was open to the sky and the tiers of seats were built on
banks of earth that formed a natural ampitheatre from
which to look out over the stage. And it was this that
had given Lee the biggest surprise of all, for it was not
the normal stage with ornate proscenium, heavy curtains and footlights that she had been used to, but a
huge elongated diamond-shaped rostrum that had been
literally built out over the surface of the lake with
only the far distant shore on the other side and the
night sky as a backcloth. The stage was built in three
tiers with narrow causeways providing entrances from
left and right with steps ascending to the central
diamond. In the distance there were floodlit fountains
that jetted liquid rainbows high into the air, and in the
centre background a full-sized replica of a galleon in
full sail rode quietly at anchor.

For several minutes Lee gazed at this unexpected
scene with unconcealed delight until Max touched her
arm. 'Shall we find our seats?'

Turning round, she saw that she was blocking the
way and hastily apologised. Once seated she smiled at
Max. 'Thank you for not telling me what it was like. It
was certainly a wonderful surprise.'

'You approve?'

'Oh, yes. But how did they build the stage out over
the water?'

'I believe they drove piles into the bed of the lake,
but I'm afraid I'm no engineer. The only drawback
with a theatre such as this is that performances sometimes have to be cancelled because of rain. But we're
lucky tonight,' he added with a glance at the clear,

cloudless sky. 'It's a perfect evening.'

As Lee looked at him she felt a strange feeling of contentment. They had kept to their truce and neither had mentioned the Alpenrose all day. Gradually she had begun to relax in his company, and Max in turn had been as charming as when he had first taken her out. His mother's presence, too, had helped, so that now Lee could even feel that perhaps it *was* going to be a perfect evening.

Soon she lost herself in the adventures of Siegfried and Brunnhilde, was captivated by the Rhinemaidens and reduced to secret tears by the tragic death of Siegfried followed by the spine-chilling funeral march. When the lights went on at last she hastily dabbed surreptitiously at her eyes with a handkerchief to remove any signs of her tears, but not before Max had noticed.

'So they moved you, those unhappy lovers?'

Lee put her hanky back in her bag and said lightly, 'Oh, I'm a sucker for sad endings. Which is stupid when it's only an opera.'

'Why is it so stupid? Aren't you as involved with the tragedy as the players? Isn't it as real to you as it is to them? Only for a short time, perhaps, but during that time it is happening to you, the tragedy is yours, so why shouldn't you weep with sorrow, or smile with pleasure when the lovers embraced, as I saw you do?' Lee flushed as he looked at her, but then he smiled, a slightly sardonic twist to his lips. 'But you English are a cold-blooded race, a race who abhor displaying their emotions, whereas we Austrians have many Latin characteristics in our temperament passed on from our Italian neighbours.'

'The only emotion I've seen you display is that of anger,' Lee pointed out. 'Admittedly you're very good at that, but I have yet to see the other side of your nature.'

'The other side?'

'The—er—romantic side,' she said demurely.

'Oh, *that* side!' There was laughter in his voice. 'What makes you think I have one?'

But he did have one, and he displayed it to perfection later that evening after they had returned to their hotel. Max had escorted them into the restaurant for supper, and at a word from him the head-waiter immediately found them a table at just the right distance from the dance floor, where they could enjoy the music but not have their conversation drowned by it. Hardly had they sat down, however, before there was a delighted cry of 'Max!' and a tall, blonde girl—who effectively reminded Lee of the Rhinemaidens in the opera—had swept up to their table. Rising immediately to his feet, Max smiled with pleasure before kissing the girl on both cheeks. Lee felt a stab of something that was almost animal in its intensity and she gripped her bag under the table until her knuckles showed white.

'Katrina! What a surprise to see you here.' Frau von Reistoven was greeting her like an old friend. 'And is Hendrik with you? Oh, yes, here he is.' She turned to shake hands with a devastatingly handsome man, about twenty-eight, Lee judged, who bowed over Frau von Reistoven's hand and murmured a conventional, '*Küss die Hand, gnädige Frau.*'

'Lee, this is Fräulein Katrina Albrich and her cousin, Hendrik Nimsgern. Our families are old friends.' The introductions were soon made and Max invited the newcomers to join them for supper so that Lee found herself seated between Frau von Reistoven and Hendrik.

'Are you staying here, Hendrik?' Frau von Reistoven asked him.

'Just for a few days, then we return to Vienna.' He

talked easily and had great charm, Lee noticed as she chatted to him, even though she was more than half absorbed in watching Max and Katrina on the other side of the table. They were talking in German, but Lee didn't have to understand the conversation to know that they were flirting with one another. That was easy enough to see from Katrina's sparkling eyes and the coquettish way she pouted or took her hand away when Max tried to hold it, only reluctantly surrendering it at last.

Lee decided that Katrina was too tall, that she was odiously coy, and that Max was a big fool to be taken in by her. She sighed; it was obvious that there was only one thing to do. With a dazzling smile she turned to a somewhat surprised Hendrik and said, 'I do *love* this music, don't you?'

She had to hand it to him, he was definitely quick on the uptake. Without a blink, he said, 'Would you care to dance, *Fräulein*?' And once on the dance floor he held her very, very close as they moved slowly round the semi-darkened room. Lee put both arms around his neck and had the satisfaction of seeing a frown on Max's face as he watched her, but then Katrina said something to him and he turned to give his companion his full attention again.

For the rest of the evening anyone watching Lee would have thought that she was having a wonderful time as she danced and laughed with Hendrik, who was only too happy to carry on a light flirtation with her and expressed his disappointment softly into her ear when the party broke up. 'It's a beautiful night. Wouldn't you care to stroll along the lakeside? We could—er—count the stars.' His lips brushed her neck and then her ear as he spoke.

Laughingly Lee refused and turned to go with Frau von Reistoven to their rooms. Then she noticed Max helping Katrina to put on her fur jacket and watched them as they left the hotel. Were they, too, going to count the stars by the lakeside?

CHAPTER SIX

AT breakfast the next day they were joined not only by Katrina and Hendrik, but also by Hendrik's father, Herr Nimsgern, who was an equally charming but older and more urbane version of his son. He and Frau von Reistoven were perfectly at ease with one another and it seemed a matter of course that both parties should join up to take a motor tour of the quaint villages and towns around the lake. At one point they boarded a ferryboat that sent up a churning wake and carried them quickly across Lake Constance to neighbouring Switzerland, which Lee was rather disappointed to find almost exactly the same as Austria. The architecture was very similar and the people spoke German at the restaurant where they went for a meal.

Hendrik hardly left her side and insisted on buying her several souvenirs, although she protested that she couldn't carry anything else.

'But surely you would like to take a fondue set back to England?'

'But really, Hendrik, I won't have room in my luggage.'

Max strolled over to them and said lightly, 'Hendrik, you must not indulge her any further or Lee will have to charter a special plane to take all these things home. Come, there's something rather special you must see.'

He adroitly led her away, but Lee bit her lip with vexation when she realised that Max probably thought she had been encouraging Hendrik to buy her presents.

The something special was a round, one-storeyed building that housed the most unusual painting Lee had ever seen. It was a panoramic oil painting which covered the entire walls of the round hall from floor to ceiling and which depicted an incident in the Franco-Prussian war when the defeated French army crossed into Switzerland in the depths of winter and asked for help for their wounded and dying soldiers. The nearer figures were life-size, the long, long column of thousands of slowly moving men, interspersed with carts of wounded and silent guns, receding into the distance. On one side there waited a train to take the wounded to hospital and Lee saw with surprise that one of the coaches was real, but it blended in completely with the picture. To stand with the painted figures all around her gave an uncanny feeling of reality, and she shivered as she saw the blood on the snow.

A hand, warm on her suddenly cold arm, made her turn to find the others gone and not Hendrik but Max looking down at her. 'It's incredible,' she told him. 'Everything seems so real, as if you expect the soldiers to start talking and moving again at any second.'

'A moment of suspended animation?' He looked round at the picture. 'Yes, I see what you mean. An instant in history has been taken and held for ever. But surely that is what a painting or a photograph is for, isn't it? But you're cold, let's go out in the sunshine again. I'd forgotten that you were—how did you put it?—a sucker for sad endings,' he said with a quizzical smile.

Dinner was eaten on the ferryboat going back to Austria, then Max drove them all back to Bregenz in the big grey Mercedes. There they said their goodbyes, for Max wanted to make an early start in the morning as he had to attend a meeting in Ausbach in the afternoon.

After their return Lee took advantage of Max's absence to slip out of the Schloss, but Rudi spotted her and came running to catch her up.

'Lee, where you go?'

'Only to the chalet,' Lee told him. 'I want to make sure it's all right.'

The house looked as deserted as when she had left it. The bowl of water that Max had used to bathe her arm still stood in the kitchen and she automatically emptied it and tidied up a bit. Going to the chimney stack, she tried to find any trace of damage, but could see nothing, nor on the bedroom side. With mounting suspicion that Max had tricked her, she climbed up the stairway to the upper floor—and then stopped in dismay. The top four feet of the stack had come loose and had slid several inches sideways. The heavy stones now hung suspended over the room in imminent danger of slipping the rest of the way and crashing down on to the floor. And the floor was all there was between the stones and the recess where she had been sleeping!

Feeling slightly sick, she locked up the house again and went to sit by the horse trough while she watched Rudi play at cattle-rustlers among Farmer Schneider's cows. So Max had been telling her the truth. The stones must have come loose during the storm and it was now obvious that the stack would have to be mended before anything else could be done to the house. Worriedly she wondered if she would have enough money to cover the cost. Her parents would, she knew, be happy to help her, but they lived on a fixed income and in these inflation-racked times found it hard enough to manage themselves. There was also Richard, but Lee knew quite definitely that she couldn't ask

Richard. Not now, not when she was so catastrophically attracted to Max.

It was no good pretending to herself; she had been jealous as hell of Katrina, had wanted desperately to be the one Max had held in his arms, had looked at under half-closed lids as he flirted so charmingly. Never before had Lee's emotions so completely taken control of her. She ached to be near him, wanted nothing more than to be beside him, but at the same time she did want more, much more! Irritably she got to her feet and started pulling the weeds away from the trough, but this made her wrist ache and she had to give up. Damn Max! Why did he have to come into her life and upset everything when her life had already been mapped out before her—a life of peace and gentle progress in a suburban house in England with Richard.

Lee sighed. Whatever came of this—this feeling for Max, one thing was abundantly plain; she would never now be able to marry Richard, never go back to take up her life in England as if nothing had happened. To try to do so would be hypocritical, not only to Richard but to herself as well. Life then would just be a sham, a façade behind which she would have to live a lie. And Max? He regarded her as a spoilt brat who had got in his way but because of her youth and sex couldn't be pushed aside as he had pushed her uncle. And was he in love with Katrina? There had been no ring on the other girl's finger, but Max had certainly showed the romantic side of his nature when in her company, Lee reflected ruefully. Perhaps in these old aristocratic continental families marriages were still arranged by the parents and there was already an agreement to unite the two families; Lee had gathered from Anna that Katrina was an orphan and lived permanently with her uncle and cousin.

She looked across at the mellowed stone turrets of

the castle set against its background of towering pin-
nacles. Was she falling in love with Max? She sincerely
hoped not, for that way lay only bitter unhappiness.
But how could she be in love with him? How could
anyone fall in love with a man they hated and des-
pised? But then why had she been so overwhelmingly
jealous of Katrina?

Rudi's shouts broke her reverie and she saw that he
had got carried away by his game and was starting to
frighten the cows, so she went over to stop him. The
boy came running across to her, knowing full well that
he had got away with being naughty because she hadn't
been watching him properly.

'All right, cowboy, I'm the sheriff and I'm out to get
you!' Lee joined in the game.

Rudi grinned delightedly, and Lee chased him all
the way back to the Schloss as Rudi's 'bang-bangs!' and
yells of enjoyment echoed through the mountains.

As Lee dressed for dinner that evening she reluctantly decided that the wisest thing for her to do would
be to leave the Schloss and get away from Max's disturbing presence as soon as she could, before she became even more attracted to him, like a piece of metal
that is inexorably drawn towards a powerful magnet.
But the only way she could leave at once was by agreeing to sell Max the Alpenrose estate! Could she do
that? Wouldn't it be a betrayal of her great-uncle's
wishes if she did so? Far better that than to have her
making a fool of herself over his arch-enemy, Lee told
herself firmly as she finished combing her hair. As
soon as dinner was over she would ask to speak to Max
privately and then tell him of her decision. And tomorrow she would leave the Schloss and go back to
England. Once there she would have the hard, painful
task of telling Richard that her feelings had changed,
and after that ...? After that she would have to find a

new job and start a new life, pushing all memories of Austria behind her. Except—except that she knew she would never completely forget.

There were just the three of them at dinner that night, but Lee was too preoccupied with her own thoughts to pay a great deal of attention to the conversation.

'I've found you a German phrase book in the library, Lee,' Frau von Reistoven told her. 'It should be useful to you.'

'That's very kind of you, thank you,' Lee murmured, trying to think of exactly what she was going to say to Max.

'I'm sure you'll find all those phrases like "Where is my yellow suitcase?" and "A thief has stolen my umbrella" very useful when we get to Vienna,' Max said teasingly.

'Vienna?' Lee said uncertainly. 'But I . . .'

'Max! You horrid boy! It was going to be my surprise,' his mother broke in indignantly.

Lee looked from mother to son in bewilderment. 'But I don't understand. You can't possibly mean . . .?'

'But yes, Lee,' Frau von Reistoven broke in. 'Max has to go to Vienna for a week or so on business and I've persuaded him to take us with him. Vienna is such a beautiful city, it would be a great shame if you didn't see it.'

'But—but I can't,' Lee protested. 'It's really most kind of you and I'm very grateful, but the chalet . . I intend to . . .'

'As a matter of fact I was going to talk to you about the chalet,' Max interrupted. 'One of my stonemasons has completely run out of work and I'd be grateful if you would let him mend the broken stack. It would be doing me a favour not to have to search for work for him.'

Raising her eyes to his, Lee could read nothing there but polite enquiry, but she knew that he was lying through his teeth, that he could find plenty of work for any number of stonemasons. But suddenly she didn't care, didn't even stop to wonder why he was lying. She knew that now was the time to announce her decision, to tell him that he could have the Alpenrose and that she was going back to England, but all her good intentions fell tumbling around her. Instead she said calmly, 'Well, if you're quite sure he has nothing to do?'

'Good, that's settled,' Frau von Reistoven said happily. 'I will show you all the sights, Lee, while Max is busy and he won't have to act as our escort on more than two evenings.'

Max looked across at his mother sternly. 'I seem to remember that it was only once,' he reminded her drily.

'Nonsense, we will be there for nearly two weeks. You can surely spare more than one evening for your poor mother,' she wheedled, but Max only grunted non-committally. 'Well, if not for me, for Lee, then?'

'Ah, for Lee.' He turned his head to look at her, his eyes resting lazily on her face. 'Now that is different.'

Lee knew that they were teasing her, but she was filled with something strangely like elation. 'Thank you,' she said, giving Frau von Reistoven a hug, then turning to Max she repeated, 'Thank you!'

He looked at her under his lids, 'Oh, if I too am not to get a hug, the deal's off, as they say in your country.'

Slowly Lee reached up until her lips just touched his cheek. 'Thank you, Max,' she whispered. He didn't look at her directly, but she saw that his mouth twisted into a crooked smile.

Vienna was everything that Lee had imagined and much, much more. She fell in love with the picturesque old part of the town as soon as she saw it and had a wonderful time exploring the quaint cobbled streets where flowers blazed like a myriad fires against the sombre antiquity of ancient walls, where blue and white petunias cascaded over ledges, flame-red geraniums spilled out of window-boxes and rich green ivy and vines scaled the crumbling old walls.

Frau von Reistoven showed her round most of the tourist spots and Lee's pile of souvenirs mounted daily. Knowing that she wasn't going to have any further work done on the chalet, she could afford to spend some money on herself.

'But it's the height of summer!' Frau von Reistoven laughed as Lee tried on a poncho-like *Loden* cloak in a shop just off the Ringstrasse. This was traditional wear for Austrians in the winter, for it was made of sturdy woollen material that was impervious to rain, snow and sleet, and although most *Loden* cloaks were of grey or dark green material, the one Lee was trying was a rich, creamy white, trimmed with bands of red and green and fastened with large silver buttons.

'Then I shall just have to keep it until the winter,' she answered as she pirouetted in front of the mirror.

Once or twice, in between business commitments, Max came with them on their expeditions, but one morning at breakfast he surprised Lee by saying, 'I hope you haven't any plans for today, Mother, because I intend to steal Lee from you, if you will permit.'

His mother smiled. 'Not at all. In fact I shall be quite glad of a rest. Being a tourist can be fatiguing; I don't know how all these elderly American matrons that one sees everywhere can "do" so many countries in such a short time. I'm sure I would never be able to stand the pace.'

'You have to have the pioneering spirit,' Max informed her.

'Oh dear, I'm afraid that died out of our family several centuries ago, so I shall just have to spend the day resting quietly,' she said comfortably.

'Where are you taking me?' Lee asked Max.

'Wait and see. It's to be a surprise.'

'But I might need to change,' she persisted.

His eyes ran over her slim figure in a sleeveless, stone-coloured dress with a wide brown belt and matching buttons. 'You will do perfectly well. I see you've left the bandage off your wrist.'

'Yes, it's fine now.'

Once outside the hotel, Max had the doorman summon a taxi and soon they were caught up in the snarl of traffic. As they passed by, Max pointed out the splendid old Imperial buildings that had once belonged to the mighty Austrian Emperors, and told Lee something of their histories. He was a far more interesting guide than his mother, for, although Frau von Reistoven knew the history quite well, she would recite it off parrot fashion, whereas Max could create a picture that made the people who had played out their lives in the buildings come alive.

Eventually they drew up outside a large eighteenth-century building where queues of tourists were waiting to buy tickets at the entrance, but Max took Lee's elbow and steered her through a different doorway where a uniformed attendant saluted as Max produced two tickets. They went down a high, arched corridor and emerged into a huge, arena-like room with galleries resting on Corinthian pillars and white-painted walls decorated with the finest of sophisticated baroque ornamentation. Then Lee lowered her eyes from the boxes on the side of the arena and saw that the floor was of soft earth. It was this that gave her a clue, and she turned breathlessly to Max.

'It's the Spanish Riding School, isn't it? Oh, Max, how marvellous!'

He bought her a programme and when they found their seats she was able to read that the reason for there being a Spanish Riding School in the capital of Austria was because the horses were first brought from Spain in the sixteenth century and that the methods used to teach them had been established for nearly three hundred years. Soon the performance began and Lee watched in utter fascination as the white Lippizaner stallions paraded to music, high stepping, high jumping and dancing slowly in unison. The red-coated riders had complete mastery of their mounts and every horse and rider performed as one. Several of the stallions did the famous 'airs above the ground' where they jumped high into the air with their legs tucked under them, then kicked them out before landing safely on the ground.

All too soon the performance was over and Lee applauded enthusiastically. 'That was one of the most exciting things I've ever seen. Thank you so much for bringing me,' she said, turning to Max.

'Would you like to visit the stables?'

'You mean you can fix it?' Lee stared.

Max grinned. 'I think it can be arranged.'

And arrange it he certainly did, for they were greeted by the head of the school himself, and given a conducted tour of the huge stables where the horses were being groomed and watered by the men who had ridden them during the performance.

'Always it is one man, one horse,' he explained. 'When the animals first are brought from Piber, near Graz, where they are bred, they always have the same rider who teaches them all their skills.'

When Max eventually told her it was time to go, Lee turned reluctantly away from the horse she had been stroking and thanked their guide warmly. Smilingly he presented her with a small medallion depicting a stallion performing one of the famous jumps. From the school Max took her across a tree-lined square, down a side street and into the discreet entrance of a café. The decor inside reminded Lee of pictures she had seen of old English coffee houses, but the sound of a zither played in the background could have come from nowhere but Vienna.

The head waiter bustled up to them. '*Guten Morgen*, Herr Doktor,' he greeted Max.

'*Gutten Morgen*, Herr Ober.'

They were conducted to a small table and presented with menus.

'Why did he call you Herr Doktor?' Lee whispered.

'Everyone who has a doctorate degree in any field is always addressed as Herr Doktor,' Max told her in a normal voice. 'Now, what would you like to eat?'

Lee looked at the menu; it was entirely in German. Heavens, she thought, I shall have to have wiener-schnitzel again, it's the only dish I recognise.

Max saw the dismay on her face. 'Perhaps you would permit me to order for you?' he offered.

Lee nodded and he reeled off a whole stream of German that turned out to be a cold soup followed by highly spiced mixed meats, grilled, and then served on long skewers, which Max said was a Balkan dish called Zigeunerplatte. For dessert they had the most delicious Apfelstrudel Lee had ever tasted.

'What do you think of the wine?' Max asked.

'I like it. It has a fresh taste.'

'I'm flattered. This is the wine we produce from the vineyards near here that I shall be visiting next week.' He looked at her and said slowly, 'Perhaps you would care to come with me?'

His expression was completely non-committal, but

Lee gripped her glass tightly as she said, 'Thank you, I'd like that.'

They finished their meal with Einspanner; large glasses of black coffee surmounted by a layer of whipped cream, then Max called, '*Zahlen, bitte*,' and the head waiter hurried over with his bill-pad and bag of change tied round his middle. The zither player was given a tip and they were bowed out of the friendly café.

'I'm afraid I'll have to leave you after I've dropped you at the hotel. I have something very important to do this afternoon.'

But even this couldn't cloud Lee's day, and she hastened to Frau von Reistoven's sitting-room to tell her of the visit to the Riding School as soon as she got back to the hotel.

'But I knew already,' Frau von Reistoven told her laughingly. 'Max told me this morning before you came down.'

'It was a lovely surprise,' Lee said gratefully. 'I'm sure I shan't enjoy anything in Vienna as much as that.'

'Don't be too sure. I've arranged for us to go to the ball at the Opera House to celebrate the opening of the Vienna Festival.'

'A ball! That sounds great.' Lee had a sudden vision of herself dancing in Max's arms and immediately began to plan what she would wear.

'And another nice thing is that we are to have some company for the rest of our stay. Herr Nimsgern and Hendrik are already in Vienna and Katrina is arriving today,' Frau von Reistoven said with the air of one conveying happy news.

'Today?' Lee faltered, her smile suddenly becoming wooden.

'Yes, Max has gone to meet her this afternoon.'

So that was his 'something important' that he had had to hurry away for! Somehow Lee managed to keep up her usual lively manner in front of Frau von Reist-oven, but once back in her room she sank down on to the bed and took out the medallion she had been given at the Riding School. They had had such a happy morning together without even a hint of the usual sparks they struck off one another. But Max's attitude towards her had been rather avuncular, now that Lee came to think about it. In fact he had behaved rather as though he was taking a young relative out for a treat!

Lee got up and began to pace up and down the room in frustrated annoyance. Why hadn't she realised that he was treating her like a child again? But she was forced to admit that her own reactions hadn't helped any; staring in awe and wonder and getting as excited as any schoolgirl, she chided herself. And now, after doing his duty by his guest, he had gone rushing off to meet the sophisticated Katrina, who was allowed to flirt and hold hands and be taken for moonlit walks! Lee came to an abrupt halt in front of the long dressing-table mirror and found that she was trembling with emotion. She stared at herself with wide, almost fright-ened eyes. What was she doing? Working herself up into a state, behaving just as she had vowed not to do. Numbly she sank down on to the edge of the bed, gripping her hands tightly together to stop them from shaking. She had to be sensible about this, she had to! To Max she was nothing but a little English girl who had got in the way, and would never be anything more than that if his treatment of her this afternoon was anything to go by.

But did she want anything more than that? And Lee realised that she did, that—just once—she would like Max to look at her and know that she was a woman.

Impulsively she turned, picked up her handbag and made for the door. She would need a new dress to go to the ball and she was going to make sure it was a stunner!

Two nights later, however, when she again stood before the mirror after dressing to go to the ball, much of her earlier frustration had evaporated and she looked at her reflection with some misgivings. The dress was certainly stunning all right; it was of soft, silver bouclé wool, the skirt hanging in shimmering folds that outlined her slim hips and long legs, but the top ...! Not that there was much of the top. Just a halter that opened into two pleated strips of material just wide enough to cover her breasts—well, nearly wide enough if she didn't move too quickly—and which didn't meet until almost at her waist. And the back was cut similarly low.

'Wow!' For once Lee was lost for words. She had wanted to stun Max, but this . . One thing was for sure, she wouldn't be able to do anything more lively than a waltz all evening for fear of losing all the covering she had. But it was guaranteed to make any man open his eyes, even Max, that blindest of all men. Still, it might not be a bad idea to wear something over it until they actually got to the ball. Carefully she draped a black stole around her shoulders so that it covered most of the bare patches and held it tightly in place at the front before picking up her little clutch bag and going through the communicating door into Frau von Reistoven's sitting-room.

Only Max, though, was waiting for her.

'Mother isn't ready yet. Would you like a drink?'

'Please. A dry Martini.' The sight of him in evening dress had a devastating effect on her and she needed a drink to calm her feathered nerves.

As he brought her the drink Max noticed how she clutched at the stole as she transferred her bag to the other hand so that she could take the drink from him.

'Why don't you take off your stole until we're ready to leave?' he asked casually. 'It's quite warm in here.'

'No, I'm fine,' Lee said hurriedly. 'I don't expect your mother will be long. Do we have far to go?'

'It will take barely ten minutes if the traffic isn't too heavy.' He went to look out of the window, so, feeling herself safe, Lee turned to walk towards a chair. Then, completely without warning, he was behind her and had whisked the stole from her shoulders.

'Mein Gott!'

Well, it had certainly stunned him all right, but somehow the dress didn't seem to be having the right effect, because he burst into laughter as he stared at her.

Lee had read about people feeling their hackles rising, but this was the first time she had experienced it herself. 'Just *what* is so funny?' she demanded.

'You appear to have forgotten part of your clothing, or did you intend to dance with this on all night?' he grinned, indicating the stole.

'Certainly not! Let me tell you this dress is extremely fashionable,' Lee retorted, longing to knock the grin off his face.

'And I expect you paid an extremely fashionable price for it. For heaven's sake, girl, go and put on something decent.'

'I have no intention of changing.' There were two bright sparks of defiance in Lee's eyes.

'If you think I'm taking you out in that—in that piece of nothing, you're mistaken. Now go to your room and put on something respectable.'

Lee glared at him mutinously. 'I won't!'

'You're behaving like a spoilt child, Lee. Don't you realise the reaction such a dress will create?'

'It doesn't seem to have created much of a reaction in you!' she said resentfully.

No, because I'm not the kind of man who finds enjoyment in pawing silly girls. Did you think I was?' He was becoming angry now and there was a sneer in his voice.

'N-no, of course not.'

'Then go and change, there's a good girl.'

Perhaps if he had continued to reason with her instead of ordering her like a child, Lee would have obeyed him, but now she said stubbornly, 'I've already said that I don't intend to change and I meant it.'

'Why, you spoilt little brat! It's about time someone taught you a lesson. And as that fiancé of yours isn't here to do it ...' He caught hold of Lee's arm and jerked her round so that she lost her balance and fell against him, finding herself held fast by one strong arm. He pulled her down over his knee and Lee struggled wildly as she realised what he was going to do. But it was no use. He delivered two hard smacks that hurt her dignity as much as they hurt her bottom before he let her up.

'You beast! How dare you? How dare you hit me, you great bully?' she blazed as she rubbed herself. 'Why, I'd like to ...' Her hand came up to hit him, but Max caught it and propelled her towards the door of her room. He dragged her through and across to the wardrobe where he pulled out a simple blue evening dress that she had worn before from among the clothes.

Here, put this on,' he commanded.

Don't you dare order me about! If you think I'm going anywhere with you after this, you're crazy!' There were tears of rage and pain in Lee's eyes as she struggled to get free, but she suddenly realised that the top of her dress was slipping and had to hastily cover herself.

'You will take off that dress and you will come to the dance!' Max said angrily.

'No, I won't, I ...'

'Or do you want me to take it off with my own hands?' he added menacingly.

'You—you wouldn't dare!' Lee glared at him defiantly, but the defiance changed swiftly to fascinated horror as he came purposefully towards her. 'All right! All right, I'll change,' she hastily capitulated.

Max continued to tower over her for a moment as if making up his mind whether to believe her, but then he said, 'I'll give you ten minutes. If you're not ready by then I'll come and get you. And don't get any ideas about locking yourself in the bathroom, because I'll break the door open if I have to.'

Lee didn't answer or look at him, just waited for him to go, then numbly slipped out of the silver dress and began to put on another—but not the blue one. She wasn't so cowed that she didn't have some spirit left. Instead she chose a full-skirted black dress with a startling white geometric design on the bodice. For the same reason she took longer than the allotted ten minutes before she ventured into the sitting-room again. Frau von Reistoven was there now and greeted her brightly, suggesting that they left straightaway as they were rather late. Lee took good care not to look at Max and so did not catch the look of sardonic amusement he gave her as he noticed her defiance in not putting on the blue dress. She hurried to get into the waiting taxi so that she could sit as far away from him as possible and look out of the window during the drive.

Whether Frau von Reistoven had heard anything of their quarrel Lee didn't know, but her hostess kept up a cheery prattle all the way so that Lee was able to sit back and try to gather her shattered dignity. She moved uncomfortably on the seat. Max had hands to match his size and he hadn't held back any; it would be a relief to be able to stand up again. Lee looked gloomily out of the window and thought of all the things she would like to do to Max; red-hot coals and boiling oil came into it quite a lot, but whatever torture she envisaged for him didn't alter the fact that he had used her as he would Rudi, as a naughty child. I should have fought him to the bitter end, she thought morosely. Now he will always expect me to give in to him, the big brute. Still, when a man threatens to take your clothes off, you don't really have much choice. Then her sense of the ridiculous returned. Well, I wanted him to notice me as a woman, but I certainly wasn't going to *show* him! she chuckled to herself.

By the time they arrived at the Opera House her good humour was completely restored—after all, it had been a very improper dress—but she was careful to keep on ignoring Max; he needn't think that she was going to forgive him that easily!

Hendrik, Katrina and Herr Nimsgern were already in the box Max had hired for them overlooking the huge dance floor. Katrina wore a clinging dress of muted lavender shades and Lee reluctantly had to admit that she looked very lovely tonight. Then she noticed that Katrina was wearing a large diamond solitaire on her engagement ring finger!

Her greetings to them purely mechanical, Lee had been sitting in the box for several minutes before her mind recovered a little from the shock and came back into focus, but the pain of knowing that Max belonged to someone else was still there deep in her heart. Dully her eyes took in the vast ballroom with its tiers of boxes and galleries hung with flowers, the orchestra below the stage and the dancing couples on the polished floor, a sight that ordinarily would have enchanted her.

'The Viennese waltz is not like your English waltz, it's much faster and more graceful, I think.' Hendrik was sitting beside her making polite conversation. Dimly Lee realised that he had been doing so for some time.

'Do—do they play waltzes all evening?'

Hendrik laughed. 'No, that would be too much even for the Viennese! The orchestra alternates with a band and a pop group, so there is something to please everyone. But will you not allow me to teach you the waltz?'

Taking Lee's hand, he led her along the passageway behind the boxes and down the dim stairs to the vast ballroom. Already the floor was fairly crowded with beautifully dressed, bejewelled women and their evening-suited partners. Hendrik drew her into his arms and whirled her into the waltz. He was a good dancer, holding her gently but firmly and guiding her easily among the throng so that they didn't knock against any of the other couples. Lee had a natural sense of rhythm and soon got the hang of the new steps; determinedly she pushed the pain away and turned a smiling face up to Hendrik, only the dead look at the back of her eyes giving a hint of the numbing ache inside her.

Deliberately she let herself drift with the music, tried to forget everything but the dizzying, whirling gyrations of movement as the tempo quickened to a rising crescendo of sound. The music stopped with a crash of drums and there were two bright sparks of colour now in Lee's cheeks as she stood panting for breath.

Putting an arm round her, Hendrik said, 'I think we ought to have a drink.' But instead of taking her back to the box he led the way instead to a lamplit bar and found an unoccupied alcove. Lee thirstily swallowed some of the drink he had brought her and then choked as the fiery spirit hit her.

'What on earth is it?' she gasped.

Hendrik laughed. 'It's Schnapps, almost our national drink. You'll soon get used to it—and you can't possibly go home without having tried it.'

Lee was all for trying anything once, but although she finished the drink she didn't like the taste. They went back on to the dance-floor and waltzed again under the brilliant crystal chandeliers that hung down from the ornate ceiling. Once she caught a glimpse of Max dancing with Katrina; he was looking down at the blonde girl and laughing at something she had said to him, while Katrina looked up at him with what Lee could only describe as radiance in her face. Then Hendrik had whirled her round and they were gone. Lee missed a step and Hendrik laughed at her teasingly. 'You've forgotten already.'

'It must be the Schnapps,' Lee apologised.

'Or the lack of it. It takes more than òne Schnapps to really get the rhythm of the waltz. Would you like another?'

'Why not?' Lee didn't particularly want another drink, but she wanted to stay on the dance-floor even less. By the time they came out of the bar for a second time the band had changed to a pop group and they were able to let their hair down to a fast beat number. It wasn't exactly Hendrik's scene, but he did his best to keep up with Lee as she let herself go to the music, her body a sensual reflection of the hot, surging rhythm. At the end of it she had to cling breathlessly to Hendrik, the music and the drink making her head spin.

'We had better go back to the box. It must be almost time for supper,' he told her.

The others were all there when they arrived and Lee sank gratefully into a chair next to Frau von Reistoven, who said, 'Good heavens, Lee, are you exhausted already? Don't forget the dance goes on until two in the morning.'

'I shall get my second wind in a minute. It's just that I'm out of practice.' Lee tried hard to be laughing and gay, to give every appearance of not having a care in the world. Perhaps she tried too hard, for she felt Max's eyes on her and looked up to find him watching her with a slight frown between his brows. Immediately she lifted her chin and gazed back at him defiantly until the ghost of a smile took the place of the frown and he gave her a small mocking bow.

A waitress arrived with a trolley bearing their supper; a plentiful variety of food from cold soup to great, fat strawberries and a large jug of real cream. But before they began to eat Herr Nimsgern motioned them to silence. He uncorked a bottle of champagne and poured out a glass for each of them, then made a speech in German during which everyone looked at Katrina, who was standing close by Max's side. The speech ended in a toast and Katrina laughed happily and swept them all a curtsey. Max raised his glass to drink to her and then smilingly took her hand in his and bent his head to kiss it.

Draining her own glass, Lee set it carefully down on the table beside her. No one had bothered to translate the speech for her, in fact it would have been entirely unnecessary; it was perfectly obvious that she had just drunk to the engagement of the man she now knew she had fallen hopelessly in love with, to his future happiness with someone else! The waitress brought her the first course, there was more champagne and then a different wine. Lee hardly touched the food; why eat when everything tasted like sawdust? But she drank the wine and let the noise and laughter from everyone else envelop her, automatically smiling and nodding whenever anyone spoke to her.

The interminable meal was over at last. The Viennese orchestra was back again and Hendrik claimed her. They all left the box this time, Lee with a fixed smile on her face that she hoped would convince everyone that she was having a fabulous time. Looking at the whirling couples on the floor, she thought that the orchestra must have had some drink with their supper, for everyone seemed to be spinning round much faster than before. The floor was more crowded, too, and it was almost impossible to keep from bumping. Looking up, Lee found her eyes attracted almost hypnotically to the glass chandeliers, each faceted drop reflecting a thousand points of light. A great shower of balloons in every colour and shape descended from the uppermost gallery, people in the boxes started throwing streamers and there was suddenly a carnival atmosphere in the huge room.

Hendrik held her closely against him to protect her from the crush of people scrambling for balloons and little fancy hats in papier-mâché. 'Let's get out of this, shall we?' Putting his arm round her, he shouldered his way through the crowd and took her into the bar again. Here he was hailed by someone he knew and Lee found herself drawn into a group of his friends. They were nice, they were fun, and took the trouble to speak English to her. They also bought her several drinks and wouldn't take a refusal when she tried to say no. But at least they didn't insist on her having Schnapps again.

It was almost an hour later before everyone filtered back to the dance. Lee felt light-headed and was glad of it; now she didn't have to think. The corridor leading from the bar was very dimly lit and a bulb had gone out, making a pool of darkness halfway along. Hendrik paused there and leant back against the wall, pulling Lee with him so that she was leaning against him.

'You're so beautiful, Lee,' he whispered in her ear.

Lee chuckled. 'How do you know? It's dark.'

He laughed into her hair. 'Oh, I know.' His lips touched her neck and then sought her lips hungrily.

She didn't particularly want him to kiss her, but some perverse instinct made her glad that one person at least found her attractive, looked on her as a woman, even if it was entirely the wrong man. Hendrik's kiss became more passionate and his hand crept up towards the bodice of her dress.

A voice as cold as ice cut across them. 'Hendrik, I think your father is looking for you.'

Languidly Hendrik pushed himself off the wall and let Lee go. Slowly she turned and found Max watching her, his expression quite unreadable in the half-light.

Hendrik went to take her hand, but Max stopped him. 'I'll take care of Lee.'

Hendrik looked as if he was going to protest, but Max said something to him in German which made the younger man look at Lee in some surprise. Then he gave her a little bow and turned up the stairs leading to the boxes.

Lee turned as if to follow him, but Max said quietly, 'You haven't danced with me yet. Shall we try this number?'

Without quite knowing how, Lee found herself held firmly in his arms, her eyes on a level with his lapel where she held them fixedly. The musicians had changed again and now a band was playing a slow, smoochy tune. Around them couples were clinging as they danced, their bodies close together, but Max held her away from him at a respectable distance.

'You seem to be enjoying yourself,' he remarked without warmth.

'Yes, I'm having a simply fabulous time.' Even to her own ears it sounded too false, too gushing.

Max's voice hardened. 'And do you always flirt with other men when you're having a good time?'

Now she raised her eyes and found him looking at her coldly, his mouth set in a hard line.

'I wasn't flirting,' she said defensively.

'No? Then just what do you call it when you let a man kiss you?'

'All right! So what if I was? It's nothing to do with you!'

'While you're my guest I'm responsible for you to your fiancé. And I hardly think he would have approved of your behaviour tonight,' he ended scathingly.

Her face very white, Lee looked blindly away. Only for a moment did she consider telling Max that she had already written to Richard to tell him that she couldn't marry him. What would be the point? It didn't matter now. Nothing mattered now that Max was himself engaged to Katrina. The music came to an end at last and Max drew her arm through his to lead her firmly back to the box. The effects of the drinks had gone completely and she just felt numb. For what little was left of the evening she sat in the box and chatted desultorily with Frau von Reistoven. Max took Katrina on the floor again and didn't come back until it was time to leave.

Herr Nimsgern's suggestion that they all go on to a night-club was immediately seconded by Hendrik, but Lee took Frau von Reistoven to one side and said quietly, 'Would you count me out, please? I've rather a bad headache. Too much champagne, I suppose,' she said wryly.

Frau von Reistoven immediately looked concerned. 'But of course. I'll take you back to the hotel and give you some pills to take away the pain.'

'No, I've some aspirin in my room. Please, I'll be all

right. Don't let me break up the party.'

'But, my dear, I can't let you go back alone.'

'I'd much rather, really. I'll put myself straight to bed and I'll feel fine again in the morning, but I'll feel terrible if I keep you from going with the others.'

Her eyes pleaded and Frau von Reistoven, sensing that she truly wished to be alone, kissed her and said, 'Very well, but I'll look in to see you when I get back.'

They dropped her at the hotel with suitable expressions of sympathy, and when Frau von Reistoven looked in on her a couple of hours later she appeared to be fast asleep, her hair across her face. Frau von Reistoven tiptoed away and Lee was free to stare blindly into the darkness again.

CHAPTER SEVEN

FORTUNATELY Max's time was almost completely taken up with travelling to neighbouring towns looking for a new warehouse site, and the evenings she supposed he spent with Katrina, so Lee saw little of him during the next few days. His mother didn't mention anything about his engagement and Lee certainly wasn't going to ask! During the long nights she lay awake, unable to sleep until the early hours. She made up her mind that as soon as they returned to the Schloss she would sell Max the chalet and go home to England. There she would tell Richard in person what she had already written in her letter. She owed him that much; that, and much more, she thought miserably. Poor Richard, it wasn't his fault that she had fallen so hopelessly for someone else. What she would do after that, she didn't know. Perhaps get a job that would entail a great deal of hard work; anything to make her forget Max. Not that she ever would; however dull the pain became in time, it would always be there deep within her. As she tossed and turned on her pillow she wished whole-heartedly that she had never given way to that crazy impulse to come to Vienna, but she had so wanted these days with Max to remember.

One evening Lee was standing at the magazine stall in the lobby of the hotel looking in a desultory way at the latest paperbacks in the hope of finding something to read that would send her to sleep, when she saw Max come through the swing doors. Hastily she turned away, but he spotted her and came over.

'Why not try this one?' he suggested, pointing to an edition of a famous but unhappy love story. 'That should satisfy your love of the sentimental.'

'Thank you,' Lee said coldly, 'but I've read it.'

'What did you think of it?'

Briefly she glanced at him. 'If you must know, I thought it was corny.' Turning away, she walked towards the lifts.

Max laughed. 'Then there's hope for you yet!' As the lift came he asked, 'Have you dined yet?'

'Yes, we ate early because your mother is visiting an invalid friend tonight.'

'Ah, yes, I remember. And you? What are you doing this evening?'

'I have several letters to write.'

'That doesn't sound very exciting for a young lady on her first trip to Vienna. Would you like to go out somewhere? To the opera, perhaps? Or perhaps you would prefer to visit one of our famous *Bierkeller*? You haven't been to one yet, have you?'

'No.' A week ago Lee would have eagerly accepted

his invitation, but now it sounded too much like an adult thinking of something that would please a child, so she said stiffly, 'Thank you, but you really don't have to put yourself out to entertain me, Max. I shall be perfectly all right on my own.'

He put a hand under her chin and tipped her face up towards him. Lee instantly lowered her lashes to hide her eyes, but he could still see the dark smudges of shadow around them.

'What, am I still in disgrace? Are you sulking because of that dress? You shouldn't make me angry, little one. Didn't I warn you that we Austrians aren't afraid to show our feelings?' His voice was softer as he added, 'Come, won't you forgive me now and let me take you out tonight?'

'I'm rather tired, and besides, Katrina . . .'

'Katrina? She and Hendrik are going to a private party tonight, so I'm afraid they won't be able to join us. Did you want them to?'

'N-no, I . . .'

'What is it? Are you afraid to come out with me? Even if I promise not to become angry with you again whatever the provocation?'

'Afraid! No, of course I'm not afraid.' She lifted her head with a touch of her old spirit.

'Then give me twenty minutes to change.' And he went off to his room, leaving Lee to wait for him with very mixed emotions.

The *Bierkeller* Max had chosen was down a quiet cobbled side street, its windows thrown open so that music could be heard coming invitingly out to welcome them. There were steps down from the entrance and a very fat, moustachioed waiter greeted Max by name and found them seats on a bench at a long wooden table where several people were already sitting. They smilingly made room for them and called out greetings while the waiter hurried to bring white wine for Lee and a large, earthenware *stein* of frothing beer for Max. In one corner a quartet of musicians played; two violinists, a guitarist who also sang, and an accordionist.

'This is the traditional *Keller* music they're playing,' Max told her, adding that it was called *schrammel* music.

Lee was content to sit and take in the atmosphere; the constant buzz of conversation, the laughter and the music that she was gradually coming to expect whenever she entered any type of eating or drinking establishment in Austria. The people next to Max had drawn him into conversation and now the young man beside Lee turned to say something to her, a friendly smile on his open face. Regretfully Lee shook her head. '*Nicht's versteh'n.*'

Over her head, Max spoke to him, explaining who she was.

'English? God save the Queen!' Which seemed to be the sum total of her neighbour's knowledge of English, but it was said with a big grin and Lee had to laugh and nod in return.

After that she no longer felt like an outsider and when the musicians sang a rousing drinking song and the people on her table joined in, linking arms and swaying to the music, she laughingly linked arms with Max and the young man and hummed along with them. Her glass seeemed to be constantly refilled, as did everyone else's, and the *Keller* became livelier as the evening progressed. Soon two men jumped into the centre of the floor and began to perform a wild *Schuhplatter* dance that was more like acrobatics than dancing, while the crowd looked on, clapping, cheering and stamping their feet as the two leaped and sprang until they were exhausted.

The heady atmosphere and the wine gradually overcame Lee and she found herself becoming very sleepy, her eyes closing as she started to nod off. She jerked herself back to consciousness, but Max had seen and said, 'I think it's time we left, Lee. You're nearly asleep.'

Regretfully she said, 'Do we have to?'

'Why, yes. You must be fresh for the morning if you want to make an early start.'

Everyone shook hands and shouted goodbyes to them as they left, showing genuine sorrow at their departure.

'You know so many people,' Lee said sleepily. 'Are they all your friends?'

'But I've seen hardly any of them before,' Max said with amusement. 'In Austria we don't keep ourselves to ourselves—isn't that the correct expression? Instead we talk to everyone we happen to meet. In the towns at the *Bierkeller*, or in the taverns when everyone goes into the country at the weekends for picnics.'

It wasn't until they were in a taxi going back to the hotel that Lee remembered to ask, 'Why did you say I needed to make an early start tomorrow?'

'Have you forgotten? I promised to take you to see our vineyards.'

Lee was silent for a minute before saying, 'Max, it was very kind of you to take me out this evening when I was at a loose end, and I enjoyed it immensely, but your mother will be free tomorrow, so I won't have to bother you again.'

'I gathered the impression that you were eager to see the vineyards?'

'Well, yes, but ... You said that you had work to do there, and I'm sure you'll be able to get on much quicker without me dragging along.'

'You're not a drag, Lee. You could never be that. So it must be my company that you don't want.'

Lee tried to give a light denial, but somehow the words wouldn't come.

'My poor girl, do you find my company so abhorrent?'

'N-no, of course not.' His eyes were gentle as he looked at her, a rueful half-smile on his lips. Oh, God, Lee thought desperately, it was hell when he was angry with her, but far, far worse when he was kind and gentle.

'It would give me great pleasure if you would come with me,' he said softly.

Perhaps it was the wine, perhaps it was because she was so tired that made her unable to keep aloof any longer. 'All right, Max, I'll come with you.'

Their journey the next morning started ordinarily enough with a taxi ride, not, as Lee expected, to the station, but to a quay on the banks of the River Danube where they boarded a large paddle-boat which carried them through some of the most magnificent scenery she had yet seen in Austria. Fairyland castles perched precariously on rocky crags on bends in the river, and below, on the banks, were the charming wine-growing villages and old market towns with their gate towers, remains of ancient walls and old houses with large bay windows and arcaded courtyards opening on to the river.

A zither was, of course, in the lounge of the boat, but they took their morning coffee on to the deck so that Lee didn't miss any of the scenery.

'I envy you your country, Max,' she remarked wistfully as they drifted by yet another red-roofed village. 'I'm so glad that I've seen it.'

'You speak as if your stay was nearly over.'

For the first time since the ball she turned to look at him fully. At his dear face, that seemed so autocratic until he smiled, at his eyes that looked at her now with a slight frown between them. 'Yes,' she answered slowly. 'It is nearly over. I think it's time for me to go home.'

Max looked as if he was going to protest, but just then the steamer hooted loudly and began to steer towards a landing jetty where they were to disembark. A smiling, dark-haired youth was waiting for them and greeted Max respectfully before leading them to a car and driving them up to the Reistoven vineyards. As far as the eye could see there were fields and fields of vines, stretching in neat, serried green ranks across the northern side of the Danube valley up to the terraced slopes of the hills until the earth gave way to rock.

The centre of the Reistoven vineyards was a French-looking house that lazed in the sun among the many outbuildings and storehouses that were needed in the process of turning the grapes into wine. Waiting to meet them were the vineyard manager, Herr Huber, and the Kellermeister, Herr Kossler, who, Max told her, was in charge of the bottling and racking of the wine in the vast dark cellars that ran deep under the house. This was one of the first places that Max inspected and Lee was invited to taste some of the wine taken from a bottle in one of the myriad racks that covered the walls.

'This is last year's wine,' Max told her. 'But most of our white wines don't have to be matured like the red clarets and burgundies of France.'

'I've never seen any Austrian wines in England.'

'No, we don't export a great deal. It's mainly purchased by hotels, restaurants and taverns here in Austria where it is sold by the glass. Wine is almost as much a part of our lives as beer.' He smiled. 'As you know.'

Lee realised he was referring to the previous evening

and smiled rather shakily in return.

Max examined the huge vats where the grapes were pressed to extract the juice, as well as all the rest of the processing plant, before they returned to the house where they lunched with Herr Huber and Herr Kossler and their wives. Between them they spoke enough English to include Lee in the conversation, but she could guess at their curiosity about her, although they were, like all Austrians, far too polite to betray it. A bleak look came into her eyes as she wondered what they would think of Max's marriage to Katrina. Well, at least she would be able to speak to them in their own language, she thought irrationally.

After lunch two horses were brought round for them and Max led her at a trot through the first of the fields of vines. Every so often he dismounted to look at the crop of grapes that were not yet fully grown; it wasn't until late August that they would finally ripen and swell in the sun. They covered a large area of ground before Max had visited all the different soil areas to his satisfaction, then he guided her to a clearing where they dismounted and he took a bottle of wine and a packet of little cakes from his saddlebag.

'Frau Huber has given us plenty to eat. She must have seen that you have an insatiable appetite.'

'Me?' Lee exclaimed, rising to the bait indignantly. 'Why, you ate like a horse at lunchtime!'

He laughed at her and spread the picnic out on the grass. 'Then you had better hurry up or there won't be any of these delicious pastries left for you.'

'In a moment.' Lee's attention had been caught by a canopied wood carving that was fixed at head height to a nearby post. Going closer, she saw that it depicted a Nativity scene, the details still sharp despite the weatherbeaten age of the wood. The craftsmanship was exquisite, as fine as any she had seen in the museums in

Vienna; there was a beauty on the Madonna's face as she looked at her child that seemed to come from the very earth about them. Slowly, reverently, Lee lifted her hand to touch the folds of the gown.

'What is it?' she queried of Max who had come to stand behind her. 'Why is it out here?'

'It's a vineyard shrine. There are many of them in the fields where the workers come to pray for a good crop or to give thanks at harvest time.' He paused, then added slowly, 'On the boat coming here you said that it was time you went home. Does that mean that you've made up your mind about the Chalet Alpenrose?'

Lee knew that she ought to tell him of her decision, that it was the perfect opportunity, but somehow she couldn't bear to see the look of triumph in his eyes when she told him that he had won the battle. She managed a rather hollow laugh. 'Don't think I'm going to give up that easily, Max. After all, I've been in Austria nearly a month now and if I don't go home soon they'll start sending out search parties for me. And I'm quite sure I can leave the supervision of the rest of the work in Herr Kreuz's hands. As a matter of fact,' she fabricated desperately, 'I've had a letter from him telling me he has a buyer who might be interested.' She turned and went to sit on the grass, careful not to let Max see her face. 'Perhaps when everything is settled Richard and I will come over here again so that I can sign the necessary papers. We might even make it our honeymoon,' she added offhandedly.

Her heart was beating fast as he slowly walked over to drop down on the grass nearby. It had been a brave lie and one that she hoped he would swallow, because she couldn't let him see how she really felt, not when she had to spend several more days in his company. And when she got back to Ausbach she would tell Herr

Kreuz to handle everything by post so that she could leave immediately for England.

'Can I have one of those cakes? I'm feeling quite hungry after all.' She managed to keep her face quite impassive as she looked at him. 'And I thought we'd agreed not to talk about the chalet?'

There was a taut, hard line to Max's jaw and he looked as if he would have liked to have said quite a lot more, but then he abruptly looked away and for the rest of the visit to the vineyards and the journey back to Vienna put himself out to talk of other, less controversial topics.

Their last few days in Vienna were spent in visiting tourist attractions they had missed earlier and in last-minute shopping, for, as Frau von Reistoven declared, heaven knows when Max would again be visiting the city. 'He has been so busy that he must have done at least two months' work in the two weeks we've been here, so I must stock up with enough clothes to last until I can persuade him to come again.'

'Couldn't you come by yourself?' Lee suggested.

'I could, I suppose, but I much prefer to have someone with me. Max usually spends much more time with me. It's unusual that he has been so busy on this visit. That's why it has been such a great pleasure to have you with me, Lee. I value your company and your friendship so much, much more than I can say.' Impulsively she kissed Lee on both cheeks and then went off to answer the phone which was ringing in the sitting-room. 'Oh dear,' she said on replacing the receiver. 'The dress I left to be altered is ready, but they want me to try it again. Will you excuse me, Lee, if I go along to collect it? I especially wanted to wear it this week-end for the dance after the festival,' she explained, referring to the village festival that was to be held in Ausbach.

'Yes, of course. I really must finish my packing, anyway.' Lee returned to her own room and the problem of finding space for all the things she had bought. She had just decided that there was no way she was going to manage without buying another suitcase, when she heard a knock on the door of the sitting-room. Going to open it she found Katrina waiting outside.

'Oh! Hallo, Katrina, won't you come in?'

'*Danke*. Is Anna here?'

'No. I'm afraid she's out. Can I help you, or take a message or something?'

'*Nein*. Is just I come to thank for wedding present.' Katrina's English wasn't very good, but it was still much better than Lee's German.

'Won't you sit down and wait for Frau von Reistoven? She won't be long.'

'I not stay. *Mein Verlobter* is wait for me in auto.'

Lee's skin suddenly began to feel tight and she felt little prickles under her skin as she tensed herself for the next question. 'Max is waiting for you in the car?'

'Max?' Katrina looked puzzled. '*Nein, mein Verlobter*—fiancé—Alvin Kleidermann. But you not met him—I forget. We marry soon. We go to live in Paraguay.'

'Paraguay!' To Lee it seemed the most beautiful place in the world and the unknown Herr Kleidermann the most wonderful person in it. She began to laugh, and after looking at her uncertainly for a moment, Katrina joined in. 'Oh, Katrina, I had you figured all wrong. You must have thought me terribly ill-mannered. I'm sure I treated you abominably, but I was so ... No, I can't tell you the real reason, but your news is the most wonderful I've ever heard and I'm so sorry if I was rude to you. Can you forgive me?' she babbled.

The blonde girl shook her head in puzzled bewilderment, so Lee laughingly caught her hand and shook it vigorously. 'I hope you will be very happy, you and Herr Kleidermann. In Paraguay.'

'*Ja, ja.*' Katrina smiled at hearing something she could understand. 'You *danke* Anna for *mein* present. I write later.'

Katrina turned to go, and when Lee came back into her bedroom after seeing her out she suddenly found that everything was spinning round so that she had to sit down quickly. To think that she had spent days and days in black despair when the engagement they had celebrated had been not between Katrina and Max at all, but with the beautiful, wonderful Herr Alvin Kleidermann! And if Katrina hadn't happened to come at the moment when she was alone in the hotel she might never have known. She might have gone back to England tomorrow without ever knowing the truth! The thought was so appalling that tears of relief came to her eyes. For a long time she sat in the chair with the knowledge that Max was free warm within her.

When Anna von Reistoven came back an hour later she found her still curled up in the chair—fast asleep.

CHAPTER EIGHT

THE drive back to Ausbach was a gay one, even though Max had thrown up his hands in horror when he saw the amount of luggage he was expected to find room for. In the end it overflowed into the back of the car, so they all rode in the front seat with Lee in the middle, a circumstance that pleased her very much. Her happiness and gaiety enlivened the journey, so much so that—

Anna von Reistoven remarked, 'You seem very pleased to leave Vienna, Lee.'

'I loved Vienna. It's a wonderful city to get to know and I wouldn't have missed it for worlds, but I suppose I'm a country girl at heart. I feel more at home among the woods and the hills than in the city streets.'

To enter her room at the Schloss was almost like coming home. Trudi was waiting for her with a big smile and helped her to unpack her many purchases, exclaiming with unenvious delight when each one was unwrapped. At length Lee came upon the present she had bought specially for Trudi. 'And this is for you,' she smiled.

At first the servant-girl was reluctant and murmured something in her own dialect, but Lee insisted and in the end Trudi was persuaded to take the small package and open it. The flush of pleasure that came over her face when she saw the bracelet inside was reward enough for Lee, but the younger girl broke into profuse thanks which Lee quickly laughed away.

'Would you finish unpacking for me? I'm going to have a swim, my first in two weeks.' Slipping into a white bikini, she hurried down to the pool, threw her wrap on to a chair and immediately dived in the deep end.

'Hey! Are you trying to drown me?'

Quickly Lee turned and found that she had just missed Max, who was floating on his back at the side. 'Heavens! I'm sorry, I didn't see you there.'

'You didn't stop to look, you mean.' Without warning he rolled over and catching her round the waist pulled her under.

'Oh, you beast!' Gasping and shaking water from her eyes, Lee looked round to take her revenge, but Max was already half way up the pool. There followed a hectic half-hour in which Max was always just a little too fast for her, eluding her hands outstretched to catch him and diving down to come up behind her and duck her again. At last she caught up with him and, putting her hands on his shoulders, used the weight of her body to draw him down to the bottom and hold him there for a few seconds until he wrapped his arms round her and lifted her to the surface. She turned a wet, laughing face up to him and his arms tightened, pulling her against him. His face was close to hers, but as Lee clung to him his smile faded and a bright, intense look came into his eyes. She felt his lean, muscular body hard against her own and for a breathless moment she thought he was going to kiss her. Instead he let go of her abruptly and swam to the side, where he sprang out easily and then reached a long arm down to haul her out.

There was nothing of his former tenseness about him as he casually offered Lee a cigarette. 'Are you still determined to go back to England soon?'

So he was reminding her of her words when they had visited the vineyards. Did that mean that he wanted her to go? she wondered.

'Your mother told me that there's to be a festival in the village on Saturday. I think I should like to stay for that, if you'll have me?'

'But of course. I'm sure Mother has asked you to stay for as long as you wish. Your company gives her much pleasure, I know.'

'And you?' Lee couldn't resist asking. 'Does my company give you pleasure?'

He smiled with genuine amusement. 'That is, I believe, what is known as a leading question. Now how am I going to answer it? Your presence in Ausbach has been disturbing, to say the least. It has caused me to lose my temper many times, even making me go so far as to be discourteous to a guest.' Lee flushed as she remembered the spanking he had given her. 'But my feelings are rather like those you felt about Vienna. It was an education getting to know you and I wouldn't have missed it for worlds.'

Now how was she supposed to take that? Really, the man was impossible! The light of battle came into her hazel eyes, but Max saw it and rose to his feet with a laugh.

'No, Lee, I'm not going to argue with you. You might tempt me to lose my temper again. Come, it's time to dress for dinner.'

Frau von Reistoven was busy helping to organise the festival for the rest of that week and Max was catching up with the work that had arisen during his absence, so Lee and Rudi were rather left to make their own amusements. Lee borrowed a car from the garage and drove round some of the neighbouring towns and villages, falling in love with the region all over again whenever she came upon a landscape that took her breath away. Twice she asked a groom to saddle a horse for her and went riding in the foothills, inevitably making her way to the chalet where she sat again by the horse-trough and looked across at the turrets of the Schloss and dreamed of castles in the air.

The chalet chimney had been expertly repaired, but there was still the hole in the roof waiting to be finished. She supposed she ought to tell Max that he had won, but she knew she wouldn't because that was the only thing that kept her in Austria. And now, more than anything else, she wanted to stay, to be near him. She didn't allow herself to hope that anything would come of it, but at least he had stopped treating her like a child; when he had held her in the pool she knew that he had been fully aware of her as a woman.

When Lee looked out of her window on the morning of the festival, she was rewarded with the promise of perfect weather. The sound of cowbells echoed through the still air and the sun caressed the valley like a cat licking its fur. Trudi came in carrying a breakfast tray, her face flushed with excitement, for all the servants were being given a holiday to attend the festival and many of them were actually taking part. Everyone was so busy that there was to be no breakfast on the terrace this morning. Both Max and his mother were leaving early to go to the village for last-minute preparations and Lee was to follow later with Rudi and the servants. After eating her rather lonely breakfast, Lee came out of the bathroom to find that Trudi had brought a large parcel and laid it on her bed.

'From Herr von Reistoven,' the maid told her.

From Max? Puzzled, Lee lifted the lid and removed several layers of tissue paper before she came upon a beautifully made Austrian peasant dress of rose-printed material with an embroidered bodice and crisp white apron. There was also an exquisite flowered headdress with gay ribbons; even the buckled black dancing pumps had not been forgotten. With trembling fingers Lee opened the card that lay on top of the clothes. 'Please wear our national costume and in doing so know that there will always be a welcome for you in Austria. Max.'

With a heart as light as air and a face just as excited as Trudi's, Lee dressed herself in the peasant costume and went to look at herself in the long mirror. How strange it felt to wear clothes that had been the traditional dress of Austrian women for hundreds of years; by just putting them on she seemed to have shed much of her modern sophistication, and the image that looked back at her from the mirror could have been that of any young village girl through the ages of time

—any girl flushed and happy at the thought of meeting her lover.

Trudi had also changed into her own *dirndl* and they went out into the courtyard together to where their transport to the village awaited them. But today it wasn't to be Hans and the grey Mercedes, instead the grooms had trundled out a huge wagonette which everyone had spent hours decorating with flowers and ferns over every conceivable surface, so that when Lee climbed into it with the rest of the women from the Schloss and took her place it was like stepping into a floral bower. Rudi was already aboard with Prinz held in his arms. He was jumping up and down and trying to persuade the young groom, Franz, who had been assigned to keep an eye on him, to let him sit next to the driver.

Two huge black carthorses, their coats brushed until they shone, and their harness adorned with countless gleaming horsebrasses, pulled them across the covered bridge, through the gatehouse and down the steep road that led to the village. Bright brass trivets with little bells suspended from them were fixed to the horses' heads so that they tinkled every time the horses moved and added to the sound of distant cowbells and the music of the alpine bands that were converging on the village square.

The wagonette rumbled slowly along, the servants exchanging greetings with everyone they met. Most of the men wore the traditional costume of white shirts, embroidered waistcoats, short leather trousers and hats adorned with sprays of flowers, but it never occurred to Lee that Max, too, would be wearing the same outfit until the wagonette pulled up in the village square and he came surging forward, head and shoulders above everyone else, to lift her out over the side, too impatient to wait for her to climb decorously down the steps. Lee gasped, not so much from being lifted down in his arms, but from the difference that his costume made to his appearance. The clothes were exactly right. She thought that they could have been designed especially for him; the soft material of the shirt clearly defined the width of his broad shoulders and the short trousers showed off his tanned, muscular legs.

But while she had been studying him, Max had also been looking Lee over appreciatively. 'You look very beautiful. The dress becomes you.'

'You look pretty good yourself.'

His mouth quirked in amusement. 'Thank you, I shall treasure the first compliment you have ever paid me,' he said mockingly. 'Come along, I've reserved a place for you where you can watch the parade.' He took her to a raised stand where Frau von Reistoven was already seated with the village dignitaries and their wives. Seats had been saved for her and Rudi and the groom a little further away.

'Rudi and Franz will take care of you and explain everything that's going on,' Max told her as he ushered her along.

Turning, Lee plucked at his sleeve. 'What about you? Couldn't you come and sit with us?'

'I'm sorry, I have to help organise the procession as it enters the village.' His left eyebrow rose slightly. 'What's the matter, don't you like Franz?'

'Well, yes, but—but I'd rather it were you.' Lee looked up at him, her eyes large and pleading, and for the first time she let something of what she felt for him show in her face.

Max gave a sharp, indrawn breath, then he propelled her forcibly towards her seat. 'Go with Rudi and Franz, there's a good girl. I have a great deal to do,' he said brusquely, then he was gone and Lee was left to join Rudi. Out of the way among the children, she thought unhappily.

The groom spoke quite good English and he began to tell her about the festival, but Lee was far too busy worrying about Max's hasty departure and whether she had given herself away to pay much attention to what Franz was saying. Soon the head of the procession, led by a band playing traditional alpine instruments as well as the more modern ones, marched into the square. They were handsome men, mostly quite young, who blew on their instruments enthusiastically and looked very dashing in their frilled shirts and black breeches tied with wide cummerbunds hung with bells. The band was followed by several men with large masks of bearded old men and over-handsome youths covering their heads. They danced along and brought squeals of delight from the children who lined the streets waving flags and paper windmills.

Several beautifully decorated lorries and carts, including the Reistoven wagonette, trundled slowly after them, then there was another band and the men who were going to enter for the various competitions that were to take place later; yodellers, alpine horn blowers, sportsmen, wood-choppers—the list that Franz reeled off seemed endless. There were more bands interspersed in the parade, all of them wearing the particular costume of their district, and among them the young people who were going to take part in the folk-dancing demonstrations, their dresses moving along the square like a river of colour, a gay kaleidoscope of rainbow tints that almost hurt the eyes by their brightness.

As the day wore on the heat became intense and Rudi began to fidget, eager to sample the delights of the fair, so as soon as the last band in the procession had passed they went to the field at the end of the village where all the stalls and sideshows had been set up. Lee, her worries temporarily forgotten, let herself be persuaded to try everything, from knocking the heads off giant effigies to bowling for a pig. They came to a spit where a huge carcase of meat was being roasted, the hot coals emitting a haze of shimmering heat, and an already extremely grubby Rudi, with Prinz tied on an old piece of cord, demanded that they try some.

'But you've already had three sausages!' Lee protested in vain.

The three of them sat under a tree to eat their pieces of ox-roast, although Lee would have preferred something more suitable for the hot, still weather. Rudi, though, ate his with gusto and plagued them for hot pancakes filled with cream from a nearby crêperie to follow.

The folk-dancing had begun and they wandered over to watch the display, enjoying every moment as the dancers skipped and hopped in the intricate set dances, swinging their partners and seemingly tireless. In between the displays the spectators were allowed to join in the more subdued versions of the folk-dances. The next dance, however, was more energetic and had one movement where the men picked up their partners by the waist and swung them high into the air amidst shrieks of delight from the girls. As Lee laughingly refused Franz's offer to take part in this, she found herself suddenly pushed forward and a voice said mockingly in her ear, 'Have you had so much to eat that you're afraid Franz will drop you?'

Next moment she was whirled up high into the air, much higher than anyone else, and then Max was twirling her round in the dance, leading her so well that she had no difficulty in following. Flushed and breathless, she skipped and spun with him until the music ended and he held her up high for a moment, laughing up at her, teasing her, before setting her lightly down.

'Phew! That was fun, but I'm so thirsty.'

'Come along, then, I'll get you a drink.' He led the way to a lemonade stall, clearing a path through the crowd easily with his broad shoulders.

'It's so hot—I'm sure they've chosen the hottest day of the year. Thank goodness the breeze has come along,' Lee remarked as she felt a cooling wind that stirred her hair and ruffled her skirts.

Max lifted his head to look at the sky, a slight frown appearing on his forehead. 'Not so good, Lee. I'm afraid it's the *Föhn*.'

'The *Föhn*? What's that?'

'It's a wind that comes from the south and blows through the Alps. Have you heard of the *mistral* in France, or the *sirocco* of the Mediterranean lands?'

'Why, yes. They can be pretty devastating, can't they?'

'I'm afraid so. The *Föhn* can be extremely violent.'

'And you think one is blowing up now?'

'Yes.' Then his serious expression changed to a smile. 'But we won't let it spoil the festival. If you've finished your drink I'll take you back to watch Mother do her stuff on the judges' stand.'

On the way they encountered Rudi, Franz having taken time off to join in the dancing with Trudi. The boy was hovering hopefully by an old-fashioned 'Try your strength' machine where several optimistic young men were bringing a huge mallet down as heavily as they could in the hope of sounding the bell at the top of a high pole. His interest in the machine became apparent when they saw that the prizes were boxes of chocolates.

Rudi's eyes lit up when he saw Max's large proportions. 'Please, you hit the bell?' he pleaded, his little face so hopeful that Max had to laugh and agree. Both boy and dog watched with fascinated expectation as Max took the huge hammer in his hands and swung it high over his head. It came down so hard that the bell clanged like a cannon-shot and frightened poor Prinz so much that he jerked the piece of cord from Rudi's hands and ran yelping through the crowd, his tail between his legs.

Lee and Max burst into laughter, but Rudi stopped only long enough to grab his box of sweets before tearing off after his pet. Max went off to help organise the yodelling competition while Lee went to watch Frau von Reistoven, who was busily judging and presenting prizes.

The fair was still at its height, an hour or so later, when Franz sought Lee out. 'Have you seen Rudi, *Fräulein*? I cannot find him anywhere.'

'Don't look so worried, Franz. After the amount he's eaten he has probably gone off to be sick somewhere. Herr von Reistoven won him a box of chocolates at the Try your Strength machine, but it made such a loud noise that it frightened Prinz and he ran away. But I'm sure Rudi must have caught him by now and is here somewhere.'

'I hope so,' Franz said with some feeling. 'He is always in trouble, that one.' He went off, and Lee continued to go round the fair alone, keeping an eye open for Rudi.

The breeze had become a little stronger now, causing the coloured ribbons on the stalls to stream gaily and the awnings to flap in the wind, but everyone was far too busy enjoying themselves to take any notice. The crowds had been augmented by coachloads of tourists from the more popular resorts, everyone good-humouredly pushing to get near the stalls and sideshows, but it was now very hot and Lee decided that she had had enough. She wanted to go back to the Schloss to rest for a while before getting ready for the dance tonight. For tonight was to be all-important; she had decided that tonight she was going to tell Max that she had broken off her engagement to Richard.

Coming away from the fairground she again encountered Franz, an anxious look on his face. 'Why, Franz, are you still looking for Rudi?'

'Yes, I'm so worried. It's nearly three hours now. Trudi is searching on the other side of the village, but I must take the road back to the Schloss. He may have gone that way.'

'No, don't do that,' Lee said quickly. 'You stay here while I search towards the Schloss. If I don't find him on the way, I'll go up to one of the turret rooms—you can see for miles from there. And I'll telephone the Hotel Erlenbach when I get to the castle. If you find Rudi leave a message for me there.'

'That is most kind, *Fräulein*, but I cannot let you. It will spoil the festival for you.'

'Now that's silly! You stay here and search around. You'll probably find him trying to con another box of sweets at the machine,' Lee said comfortingly. With a cheerful wave she set off to walk back towards the castle, pausing at every farm gate and footpath to shout Rudi's name, but there was so much noise from the festival that it was impossible to distinguish any answering call. The Schloss was deserted except for the old man at the gate when she arrived there, having seen no sign of Rudi and his dog on the way. Knowing how anxious Anna von Reistoven must be, Lee went straight to the telephone in the drawing-room and rang through to the hotel.

'Herr Gruber? It's Fräulein Summers. Has Rudi been found? No, I haven't seen anything of him this side of the village.' The innkeeper told her that Franz and Trudi had gone to search the woods near the village. 'I'll go up to the turret and see if I can see anything from there,' Lee offered. 'I'll hang up and phone you back again shortly.'

By the time she reached the topmost room in the tower she was wishing fervently that a lift had been built into it instead of the spiral stone staircase that ran up inside. Throwing open the window, she leant out and savoured the fresh air while she got her breath back. It was quiet here away from the village and she noticed that the wind had become quite strong now and was tossing the tree branches from side to side and whistling eerily round the tower in which she stood. Lifting her binoculars to her eyes, she carefully scanned the countryside. Suddenly the wind changed and brought her the faint sound she had been listening for; the frightened yelping of a dog. Yes, it came again, more certainly this time, and seemingly from the direction of a large tract of forest over half a mile away, where the trees grew so thickly that it was impossible to see anything among them. But she was sure that it must be Rudi and the dog. They were probably stuck somewhere again. She had been concentrating so closely on the trees that it was not until she drew back to run down the staircase to telephone the hotel that she saw something that made her stand frozen with horror.

On the skyline above the trees, and slightly to one side of where she thought the barking was coming from, was a threatening pall of black smoke! A forest fire! And the wind was momentarily becoming more violent and pushing the flames towards Rudi!

CHAPTER NINE

LIKE a whirlwind, Lee dashed towards the stairs and
ran down them two at a time, regardless of the possi-
bility of a sickening fall against the hard stone. Once
she stumbled, but managed to save herself and reached
the ground floor where she sped as fast as she could
across to the stables. No time to telephone the hotel, no
time to find the old gatekeeper and tell him where she
was going—every second was precious if she was to get
there in time. A bay mare whickered a welcome as Lee
threw open the stable door and pulled a hastily
snatched-up harness over its head. To strap on a saddle
would take too long, so she sprang up on to the mare's
bare back, pulling the unfamiliar skirts of the *Dirndl*
up above her knees as she kicked the horse's flanks. The
postern gate was left open behind her as she encouraged the mare with heels, knees and voice to gallop
across the fields towards the outer trees of the forest
and the fire that was every minute raging more fiercely
and nearer and nearer to the little boy trapped there.

Without bothering to look for a path through the
trees, Lee rode on through the forest as fast as she
dared, being careful to keep her head low over the
horse's neck; it would never do if she were to be un-
seated by a low branch now. Twigs cracked like pistol
shots beneath the mare's hooves; it hadn't rained since
the great thunderstorm that she had watched with Max
several weeks ago and the brushwood was dry as tinder.
Now that a fire had started nothing would stop it until

it had consumed the whole forest, Lee reflected grimly.

Prinz's frightened barking was much nearer now and she yelled Rudi's name. Immediately there was an answering shout from over to her left, and soon she was slipping lightly from the mare's back and tying it to a tree near where Rudi was ineffectually trying to scrape the dirt away from an old rabbit hole that Prinz had got well and truly stuck in. He was using a stick and his bare hands, but Prinz was struggling so wildly to escape that he was becoming more deeply embedded and had only his head protruding from the hole. But his head was making enough noise to deafen them!

It took only a quick glance for Lee to see that it would take a little time to free the dog, but the wind must have changed again, for there was as yet no sign of the fire in their vicinity, thank goodness. Stooping down, she made soothing noises to Prinz while Rudi poured out his story to her, although she paid him scant attention. With sinking heart she saw that the dog's legs were pinned beneath a tree root inside the hole, and then, for the first time, she caught the rich smell of wood smoke carried on the wind. She knew that she must get Rudi to safety, but how to make him leave the dog?

'Rudi, can you ride a horse?' she asked, pointing to the mare to make him understand. He nodded uncertainly. 'Good. Go to the Schloss,' she said slowly. 'Telephone Max at the Hotel Erlenbach.' She mimed making a telephone call. 'You understand? Get help. *Verstehen*?'

'*Ja*, I understand. But Prinz?'

Suddenly a frightened deer sprang out of the thicket and went bounding past them. Rudi looked round and then he, too, smelt the smoke. '*Ist* fire! Prinz will be burned!' His voice was high-pitched with fright and he clung desperately to Lee's skirts.

'No, I'll get Prinz out. You go to the Schloss.' Lee
lifted him on to the mare's back and used the cord from
round Prinz's neck and the apron from her costume to
tie him on as firmly as she could. 'Don't worry about
Prinz, I'll bring him. Remember to keep your head
down and hold tight. The mare knows the way.' Hoping that he understood, she gave him a quick hug and
sent him on his way with a smile.

But as soon as he was out of sight she turned hurriedly back to the puppy. The fire was still some way
off and she should have enough time to get the dog
out of the hole and run to the edge of the forest before the fire reached them, but there was no time to be
lost. Tearing the buckles from her shoes, Lee used them
to enlarge the hole, knowing that she wasn't strong
enough to break the roots that held him. As she worked
small woodland creatures hurried past in increasing
numbers; rabbits, marmots, hedgehogs, and once or
twice a chamois, its usual extreme shyness forgotten,
raced past them heading for the safety of the mountains.

As Lee dug deeper the soil became harder and her
hands were cut and bleeding from the sharp edges of
the buckles. Prinz, sensing the danger, had become
quiet, merely whimpering and licking her hands whenever they came near him.

'Yes, boy, I know you want to get out of there, but
I'm doing my best.' Eventually she was able to get a
good hold on him and, with much pulling from Lee
and much scrabbling from the puppy, he at last came
free. 'Phew! Only just in time, I think.' Afraid that if
she left the dog to run beside her he might get caught
down another hole, Lee picked him up and began to
run in the direction she had come.

Despite the uneven ground and her heeled shoes, the
smell of smoke became fainter as she hurried along

and she became increasingly confident of getting to safety in plenty of time; almost she wished that she hadn't sent Rudi to telephone for help because she didn't want to start an unnecessary alarm or get the child into a row. She ducked her head to pass under a low tree when, without warning, a small herd of deer crashed past her at an angle, their terror of the fire sending them thudding against her. Desperately Lee tried to turn aside, but as she did so the heel of her shoe caught in a root and the next moment she found herself rolling dizzily down a steep slope, the frightened dog still clutched in her arms. Brambles and undergrowth tore her clothes and the headdress from her head as she tumbled, her shoes falling off her feet as she struggled to stop herself. Then her head struck a protruding piece of rock and a sharp, numbing pain shot through her head before she lost consciousness.

Something warm and damp kept touching her face. Vaguely Lee wondered why someone was trying to wash her face when she was asleep and she tried to move her head away, but this hurt so much that she gave a cry of pain. Slowly she put a hand to her head and felt a large bump. 'Oh, my head!' Dizzily she sat up and Prinz immediately barked with delight and tried to lick her face again. 'It was you, was it? Hey, okay, you're a good dog, but I'm fine now.' Lee pushed him away and struggled to her feet, then started to cough. Slowly, sickeningly, she realised that there was thickening smoke all around and she could distinctly hear the crackle of the fire behind her. Then, only a hundred yards away, a tall pine burst suddenly into flames, its branches swallowed in seconds by the blaze.

Panic-stricken, Lee's only instinct was to do as the animals had done and turn to run before the fire, but she had enough sense to tear a piece of material from

her skirt to tie over her nose and mouth; she knew that
the smoke could be just as deadly as the flames. Snatch-
ing up Prinz, she tried to run as fast as she could, but
the pine needles stuck in her bare feet and she kept
blundering into trees because the gusts of smoke made
her eyes water. Prinz was struggling and barking with
terror in her arms and at last, completely exhausted,
Lee let him jump to the ground while she leaned
against a tree trunk, gasping for breath.

'Go on, go home, boy,' she panted. 'Go home, Prinz!'
But the little dog only barked louder than ever and
tried to leap up her. 'No, Prinz, go home. Go find Rudi.
I can't carry you any longer.'

All at once a huge shape loomed up out of the smoke
and Lee gave a cry of terror as she remembered that
bears sometimes came into these forests. The shape
came nearer and Prinz turned to bark defiantly, but the
last of Lee's courage deserted her and she sank cower-
ing to the ground.

Then, unbelievably, she felt herself picked up in two
strong arms and looked up into Max's anguished eyes.
'Lee! Are you all right? Oh, *meine Liebling, meine
Geliebte*! I was afraid I would never find you!'

Lee tried to answer, but could only cough. The next
instant Max had lifted her on to the broad back of the
quivering black stallion and was about to leap up behind her when Lee pointed desperately to Prinz. 'Don't
leave him. Please, Max,' she gasped.

Quickly he turned and scooped up the dog, dropping
it into her lap, then he was behind her, his arms like
mighty bastions as strong as the castle walls to protect
her from danger. He seemed to be making for higher
ground, the frightened horse held firmly in check by
his iron hands, and soon they came to a wide ride cut
through the forest. They turned to make for the edge
of the woods—but they were too late! They had only

gone a little way when the freak wind threw burning sparks ahead of them and they found their way completely cut off. *'Verdammt!'* Max cursed fluently, turned the horse round and headed in the opposite direction.

'But, Max, the fire is worse this way!' Lee turned frightened eyes up to him.

'Trust me, little one.'

Then she wasn't afraid any longer. She had complete faith in him and if he wanted to go that way then it was all right by her. Before long he jumped down and pulled off his shirt, tying it securely over the stallion's eyes so that the flames which were now rapidly closing in on them wouldn't terrify the animal into blind panic. Then he climbed up again and, taking the reins from Lee, dug his heels into the horse's sides and pushed him into a canter. The blaze on either side came even nearer as Max broke into a gallop and to Lee it seemed as if they were thundering down a long tunnel of fire. The heat was intense and she could hardly see, but suddenly she gave a cry of warning. A tree had fallen across the ride ahead of them!

Max didn't hesitate but gathered the horse and gave a yell of encouragement as the magnificent beast jumped clean over the blazing trunk. Still they went on, and Lee wondered frantically if Max was trying to take them through the fire to the other side of the forest, but then she heard him give a cry of triumph as they broke through the flames and dashed headlong into a mountain lake.

The water was icy cold and very deep, so that soon the horse was swimming in the direction of a small island in the centre. Other animals, too, had sought refuge here, and as they climbed up the bank rabbits and squirrels darted away into the trees and shrubs that grew there. Max lifted her and Prinz down and while he tied the stallion to a tree she turned to look behind her at the fire. It seemed impossible that they could have come safely through such a holocaust; even now a great pine, its branches a living bonfire, came crashing down to completely block the ride. If they had been a few minutes later!

Putting her hands over her face to shut out the mental pictures, she began to shake uncontrollably.

'Lee, my dear one, don't cry. You're safe now. Safe with me.' Max's arms came about her and Lee felt the hairs on his bare chest soft against her face.

'Oh, Max! Max, I was so afraid!' Lee clung to him tightly, his warmth and nearness giving her strength and comfort. She raised her face to him, love taking the place of fear in her eyes. Her hands came up to touch his face. He gave a little moan, and then his lips were on hers avidly, exploring, seeking, filling her body with a longing she had never known before. Ecstatically she returned his kiss and his lips became more passionate, more demanding as he held her close against him. His mouth sought the curve of her chin, the hollows of her cheeks, her neck, her eyes.

'Max. Oh, Max,' she gasped as she moved against him, lost to everything but the aching need she felt for him. Slowly she became aware that he had drawn away and was standing perfectly still.

'I'm sorry,' he said harshly. 'I shouldn't have done that.'

'But—but why?' Lee stared at him confusedly, unable to take in the sudden change in him.

Max's voice was suddenly savage. 'You ask me why? Because I have no right to kiss you—to touch you! Because you're promised to another man, that's why!'

'Max, I ...' Lee tried to speak, but he wouldn't listen.

'By kissing you like that I was behaving worse than

Hendrik—at least he didn't know you were already engaged. But I do.' He stared down at her, a dark, desperate look in his eyes.

'Max, if you'll just . . .'

But again she wasn't allowed to finish, for he lunged forward and caught her to him again. 'Oh, *Gott*, it's no use! I can't hide how I feel for you any longer. Lee, *meine Liebchen*, you can't marry him, I won't let you. He doesn't deserve you,' he added forcefully, and kissed her again.

'If you'll just listen to me for a moment!' Lee somehow pushed herself away from him and looked up with shining, misty eyes. Tremulously she said, 'Max, I'm not going to marry Richard. I wrote and told him so when we were in Vienna.'

He stared at her incredulously. 'But it was in Vienna that you said . . .'

'I know what I said,' Lee interrupted, 'but it wasn't true. I only said it as a kind of—of defence.'

Almost as if afraid to ask the question, he said slowly, 'Why, Lee? Why did you say it?'

'Because—because I thought you were going to marry Katrina, and I didn't want you to find out that I . . .' She lowered her head and then raised it again to look steadily into his eyes. 'That I was so very much in love with you.'

Slowly Max raised his hands to cup her face. He looked at her like a blind man who could suddenly see for the first time, as if he were memorising every detail of her face. 'My dearest love,' he said softly. His lips brushed against her throat, the softness of her cheek, the lobe of her ear, her eyes, never quite touching her mouth, all the while whispering endearments. 'My little love, my darling. Oh, Lee, *ich liebe dich*! I love you so much, my dearest. Can you ever forgive me? I've bullied you and made you unhappy. I think I fell in love with you the first time I saw you, but I tried so hard to fight it that I was rude and overbearing and made you hate me.'

Lee smiled tremulously up at him. 'I did at first, but ...'

'But now?'

'I'll never love anyone but you,' she said simply.

With a little sound of triumph Max crushed her to him and this time sought her mouth greedily. 'Lee, *Liebchen,*' his voice was thick. 'I tried so hard not to love you. It was pure hell, with my instincts in turmoil— wanting you, yet knowing that you could never be mine. But I couldn't keep away from you. I had to see you! I was even glad when you hurt your arm because then I could have you near me, see you every day, even though seeing you was exquisite torture.' He pressed her close against him, but it wasn't close enough. The weeks of longing were over and she moaned as his hands touched her body, exploring, caressing.

'Why on earth didn't you tell me you had broken your engagement?' he said at last, his eyes still slightly glazed.

'I wanted to, but—I didn't know whether you cared,' Lee said slowly as she remembered the agonies of un-happiness.

His hands gripped her shoulders tightly. 'Oh, I cared. You'll never know how much I cared.'

'So why don't you show me?' she said softly as she ran her fingertips gently across his shoulders and down through the silky hairs on his chest.

A light flared in his eyes as he pulled her fiercely to him, and it was only when the stallion neighed with fear that he let her go and turned to see that a spark had blown across the lake to set light to some under-growth on the island. Quickly he ran across and stamped it out.

'You'd better try and get some rest,' he advised her. 'We won't be able to leave here until the fire has burnt itself out and the forest has cooled down.'

He found her a place to sit against a rock, but himself tirelessly patrolled the little island, ready to beat out any spark that blew in their direction, guarding them, keeping them safe. Prinz came to snuggle in Lee's lap, gently licking her hand before settling down to sleep. But she couldn't sleep; the conflagration that now completely surrounded the lake was too frightening. It wasn't until the fire had passed and there was no longer any danger of flying sparks that Max came to sit down beside her. Happily, trustingly, she then pillowed her head on his shoulder and was soon asleep in his arms.

The *Föhn*, the terrible wind that had caused the fire to spread so relentlessly, had at last blown the smoke away as the fire burnt itself out, and the orange glow in the sky was giving way to the grey dawn of a new day as Lee awoke. None of the forest had been spared. It had been killed overnight and would lie black and dormant for a long time before new shoots would start to push their way through the ashes to the light of the sun. But some of the small creatures, restless for their homes, were already slipping quietly into the water and swimming back to the shore.

Lee stirred and realised that Max was no longer beside her. Sitting up, she saw him down at the water's edge looking across at the blackened forest. Quickly she got to her feet and ran to him, eager to be near him, wanting to feel the reassurance of his hand warm on hers.

He took her in his arms and held her close before saying teasingly, 'You realise that we've spent the night together, don't you? Now you'll have to marry me so that I can make an honest woman of you.'

'I shall insist on it!' Lee retorted happily as she drew his head down so that she could kiss him.

'And the Chalet Alpenrose?' There was a slightly anxious look that he couldn't disguise in his eyes as he asked the question. 'I have papers at the Schloss. I'll show them to you when we get back. Old Herr Staffler has hated my family ever since my grandfather's day. It was he who poisoned your great-uncle's mind, making him think that all his ills were our fault, just as he tried to poison yours—but, Lee, I can ...'

Lifting her hand, Lee placed her fingers over his mouth to stop him. 'It doesn't matter any more, Max,' she said softly.

He turned his head into her palm and kissed it gently. 'I don't want it ever to come between us again, Lee,' he said earnestly.

'It won't, because I've decided to give the chalet away.'

'Give it away?' Max's eyebrows rose in astonishment.

'Yes,' Lee smiled. 'To you—as a wedding present.'

There was something like relief in his laughter. 'So the estate that was taken as a dowry will be restored as a dowry. Very fitting!'

Looking across the lake, Lee asked, 'Is it safe to go back now?'

'I'm going to swim across to find out. Will you be all right here for a little while?'

At Lee's nod Max sprang across the stallion's back to urge the horse into the water. Lee followed him to the edge and tried to wash off some of the smoke and grime, using a flounce torn from her petticoat. There really wasn't much of the pretty Tyrolean costume left now, she realised sadly.

After about twenty minutes Max splashed back on to the island, his chest blackened by charred wood. 'We should be able to make it. I had to move some debris out of the way, but I think we will be safe enough if we can get through the ride.'

As he lifted her gently on to the horse's back, Lee looked down at him, her heart full of love and pride, but then she was swept with a strong feeling almost of fear so that she clung to his hand.

'Lee, what is it?'

'Nothing.' She shook her head. 'It's just that I'm so happy and I was suddenly afraid that something might —might happen to spoil it.'

'Nothing is going to happen, *Liebchen*,' he said softly, then added with a grin, 'Not when you have a king-sized moron to protect you!'

Lee laughed. 'Oh, dear! Will you ever forgive me for that?'

'I might. But only after you've atoned quite a lot, of course,' he added with a look that brought a blush to her cheeks.

He swam along beside them across the lake, then led the stallion into the entrance of the ride; the tree he had shifted out of the way lay to one side and Lee saw that it must have taken all his considerable strength to move it, even charred and blackened as it was. Ashes lay inches deep on the ground and sent up puffs of acrid soot beneath the stallion's hooves as Max led them slowly along.

It made Prinz sneeze and Lee stroked him gently. 'Never mind, little dog, you'll soon be safe with your master.'

Max turned his head at her voice and for a long moment their eyes met and held, the knowledge of the fiery hell that had so nearly claimed them strong in their minds.

More fallen branches impeded their progress, but Max's powerful muscles lifted them easily out of the way, but once he gave a gasp of pain as he unknowingly went to lift a branch that was still smouldering.

'Have you hurt yourself? Let me look.'

'It's nothing.'

'Don't be silly, Max, let me look at it.'

He lifted his hand to show a large burn on his palm. Tearing off the last remnants of her petticoat, Lee fashioned a pad to protect the wound and tied it securely in place. Silently he nodded his thanks and they proceeded on their way along the ride. They came out of the forest at last, much higher up than where Lee had entered the previous afternoon, and she suddenly realised that it was going to be a beautiful day. The wind had gone completely and the sun shone brightly down on the sheep and cattle in the fields, their bells sending a cheerful cacophony ringing through the hills. It all looked so peaceful; just as if the fire had never been.

Slipping the reins over his arm, Max raised his hands to his mouth and sent a yodelling cry echoing down into the valley. Immediately there was an answering call and soon several figures came in sight, running towards them. Shouts of delight and relief reached their ears long before the men were near enough to be recognisable. One of the first was the young groom, Franz, but he stopped short when he saw them, a mixture of shock and horror clearly written on his face. Lee realised that they must look a dreadful sight; Max was black from head to toe and, although she had washed herself at the lake, the clouds of soot had made her filthy again, her clothes were beyond recognition and her face, arms and legs were cut and scratched from where she had fallen. There was also a large bump on her head that ached abominably.

Everything seemed to happen at once then. She heard Max's voice giving orders and he lifted her down and carried her across the meadow to a lane and a waiting car. Someone tried to take Prinz from her, but she clung grimly to him; she had saved him for Rudi and she intended to part with him to no one else. When the car drew up in the lovely courtyard of the Schloss, Anna von Reistoven and Rudi were there waiting. Rudi came scurrying across, the biggest grin on his face Lee had ever seen. With a little smile she handed him the puppy. He gave her a big, sloppy kiss and went dashing off out of the castle, excitedly shouting the news.

Anna ran first to Max and held him close, tears of relief in her eyes. Then she turned to Lee, her arms outstretched. '*Gott sei Dank*, you are both safe! But you must be exhausted. Max, take her to her room quickly. Frau Muller, ring for the Doctor. Run ahead and prepare a bath, Trudi.'

Lee could have walked to her room, but Max insisted on carrying her and she definitely wasn't going to argue. Languorously she turned her face into his bare neck. The scent of wood smoke still clung to his skin and she knew that she would never again smell the aroma without remembering this moment. Then she was in her room and Max was gone, leaving the women fussing round her. Stepping into the bath was a small hell of pain, but Trudi helped her and it felt good to be clean again and to have ointment smeared on her cuts and grazes. The doctor dressed them for her and gently felt the bump on her head. 'I'll give you something to take the pain away and make you sleep,' he told her.

Nodding obediently, Lee took the pills he gave her. Exhaustion overcame her and she fell asleep, but instead of dreaming happily of Max, strange visions began to torture her mind; she was back in the fire, Max was riding off and leaving her. She cried out to him, but he wouldn't listen, wouldn't come back. She awoke, screaming, to find Anna von Reistoven beside her, holding her tightly in her arms.

'It's all right, Lee, you're quite safe now. The danger is all past, my poor child.'

Slowly Lee came back to reality and clung shamelessly to Anna, shudders of fear still shaking her and beads of perspiration running down her flushed face. Trudi brought her a cool drink and she lay back against the pillows still gripping Anna's hand tightly. But she was too afraid that she would have another dream to go to sleep again for a long time.

When next she awoke the curtains were open and bright sunlight filled the room, little dust motes hovering in the shafts of light. For a puzzled moment she thought that she must be in the garden, for there was a strong scent of flowers in the air. Lifting her head, she looked round and saw vases and bowls of flowers everywhere. Lee smiled happily, knowing who had sent them and the message that went with them. Quickly she got up and was about to start dressing, but Anna poked her head round the door and firmly ordered her back to bed.

'No, Trudi will bring you some food and I'll stay and keep you company.'

The older woman stayed with her, talking gently. 'We didn't know that you had even left the festival until Herr Gruber became worried because you hadn't telephoned again. He contacted Max and told him what had happened, so Max drove up here straightaway. He found you and the mare gone and the postern gate open. One look at the skyline was enough to send him galloping after you. *Gott sei Dank*, he found you! But I'm telling you what you must already know. Max must have told you all this when you were on your little island.'

'No, he didn't. Er—he was busy putting out all the

sparks, you see.' Lee found herself flushing and hastily lowered her head.

'Ah, yes, I understand.' There was amusement in Anna's voice until she went on more seriously, 'Well, Max met Rudi on the way and sent him to raise the alarm while he went to look for you. All the men from the village came and tried to help, but the fire was burning so fiercely that it couldn't be contained. We could only hope that Max's knowledge of the forest would save you. It was the longest night I have ever spent in my life!'

'Oh, Frau von Reistoven!' Impulsively Lee kissed her hostess, knowing how afraid she must have been, what terrible pictures must have been chasing through her mind all the time Max was missing.

For a moment they clung together until Anna said, 'But this won't do. We are being silly women. You are both safe, and you must eat and recover your strength. It has been a great shock to you, I know.' She settled Lee into the bed and tucked her in. 'Ah, here's Trudi with your food. I must go and see Max. I have an idea he may have something very important to tell me,' she added mischievously before kissing Lee lightly on the forehead and going quietly from the room.

Trudi hovered by her as she ate, excitedly telling Lee how they had almost been given up for dead. 'Everyone said it was very foolish of Herr von Reistoven to go after you,' she chattered on, Lee only half listening. She was longing to see Max, yearning to feel his arms round her again and know that it was really true, that the miracle had happened and she was going to be his wife.

'They said that he would never find you,' Trudi went on, and after more in this vein, added, 'But perhaps, now that he has saved your life, you will sell him the Chalet Alpenrose. Then the Government will give him a great deal of money so that they can build the new *Autobahn* through the valley, and Herr von Reistoven will build the new hotel he plans and ...'

'What—what did you say?' Lee murmured, her brain only just taking in what the maid had said.

Trudi broke off and put her hand to her mouth in dismay. 'Oh, I'm sorry! Herr von Reistoven said I mustn't tell any ... I shouldn't have said that. I must go back to the kitchen now.' Agitatedly she turned to hurry to the door.

'Trudi! Come back!' Lee was out of bed and had caught her by the wrist. 'Trudi, you said that Max— that Herr von Reistoven planned to build a hotel on the site of the Chalet Alpenrose? That there was going to be a road cut through the valley? Is this true?'

The girl mumbled something in her own language and tried to pull away, her eyes not meeting Lee's.

'Trudi, you must tell me the truth. You've got to!' Lee said desperately, her heart sick with fear—fear that her happiness was about to fall in ruins round her feet.

Slowly the maid said, 'Yes, it's true, but please don't tell Herr von Reistoven I told you. No one else knows. It was only because I overheard him talking on the telephone.'

'What did he say?' Lee asked urgently. 'Please, Trudi, you must try and remember exactly what he said. Do you understand?'

The maid nodded, frightened by Lee's vehemence. 'It was before you came to Ausbach but after Herr Canning had died. Herr von Reistoven came into his study to answer the telephone when I was cleaning the windows. He didn't see me because I was partly hidden by the curtain. I think the call was from his solicitor in Vienna, because he mentioned Herr Linz who comes here sometimes.'

'Yes, yes, but what did he *say*?' Lee urged her.

'He said that Herr Canning had died and that the solicitor was to find out the terms of his will and try to buy back the Chalet Alpenrose estate. Then he listened for a little while to the other man, then he said, "It will give us the land we need to complete the toll road. The government will have to give us a percentage of every toll and we will have the franchise for the only hotel and garage. It will make a vast profit."' Trudi paused. 'That is the translation, you understand, but my English is very good, I think.'

'Yes, Trudi,' Lee said dully. 'Your English is extremely good.' She turned away. 'Will you take the tray away, please, I don't feel hungry any more.'

Relieved to get off so lightly, the maid picked up the tray but hesitated at the door. 'Please, *Fräulein*, you will not tell Herr von Reistoven that I have told you? When he saw me by the window he made me promise not to tell anyone.'

'No, I won't tell him.' Trudi hurried from the room and Lee crossed to the window to gaze out at the now familiar scene. The sun still shone brilliantly, but for her the warmth had gone out of the day. She had been such a fool, such a blind, gullible fool! She ought to have known that someone in Max's position would never offer to marry her for herself alone! All he had wanted, had ever wanted, had been the Alpenrose estate, because it was worth a small fortune to him. Without it the pieces of land on either side would be useless; with it he had full bargaining power. And even without the tolls from the road, a hotel situated in the chalet's position, in the most beautiful part of the valley, would be an extremely successful business venture in itself. No wonder he had fought so hard to get it, she thought bitterly. How furious he must have been when she wouldn't sell to him, and how even angrier when she had taunted him with her ability to fight him in the courts through Richard.

So then he had got desperate, decided that the only way to get what he wanted was to take her as well. And she, poor lovesick fool, had played right into his hands, she realised with bitter self-irony. Oh, he had been very clever about it, taking her to the opera and being charming to her one moment, and then making her jealous by flirting with Katrina the next. And when he had seen her reaction he had played on it, sometimes being attentive to her, sometimes keeping out of her way so that she was always unsure of herself. She realised now that he could easily have told her of Katrina's engagement, but he had deliberately let her go on thinking that it was he who was engaged to the Austrian girl, probably hoping that she would give up hope, sell him the chalet and go home. And how close she had come to doing just that! Then he would never have had to sacrifice himself by marrying her, she told herself with savage self-contempt.

And when he had kissed her during the fire? When he had held her close and told her he loved her? Were those, too, all lies? Lee closed her eyes and gripped the window frame until her fingers hurt. No, perhaps some of it had been true, because he wanted her, she knew. Perhaps to possess her sexually would be an added bonus on top of everything else! It was easy to see now why he had been so quick to ask her about the chalet before they had left the island, and she had so happily —so besottedly!—said exactly what he had wanted to hear. Unable to bear her own thoughts, Lee turned away from the window, her eyes dark with hurt and self-reproach.

Slowly she began to dress, not caring what she put on, while her numbed brain tried to sort out what she was going to do. Lingeringly she touched a piece of old furniture and an exquisite ornament. How quickly she had come to love this place, to feel secure within the warmth of its protecting walls and to delight in its treasures which were such an intrinsic part of the whole. It would be hard to leave, but impossible to stay. That she couldn't stay was obvious, but how to get away without having to face Max? For she never wanted to see him again; not now, not when she knew him willing to do anything for money and power, even go so far as to sell himself.

As she bent to put on her shoes, Trudi knocked and came in.

'*Fräulein*, there is a visitor for you,' she said, her face alight with curiosity. 'His name is Herr Derrington. He is waiting in the small library.'

Lee stared at her. Richard! Richard here! 'Thank you, Trudi, I'll come at once.' Then she added quickly, 'You needn't bother to tell Herr von Reistoven.'

As she hurried down the corridors and stairs, Lee's heart began to beat wildly. She knew why Richard was here, of course. He had come in answer to her letter breaking off their engagement. But could she ask him to help her now? Help her to get away from the Schloss without seeing Max? Pushing open the library door, she paused uncertainly in the doorway. Richard turned from examining the bookshelves and faced her. He looked so familiar, so *safe*. Lee pushed the door shut behind her and ran across the room to bury herself in the haven of his arms.

'Oh, Richard!' She knew he would comfort and take care of her, and that she needed more than anything right now.

'Lee! What is it?' He saw her eyes like two dark, burnt-out embers in her desolate face. 'Why, you're shaking. What the hell have these people done to you?' His voice was so full of concern that Lee could have put her head on his shoulder and wept, but she bit her lip and stood away from him.

'Oh, Richard, I'm so glad to see you, you've come at just the right time. I need your help so badly.'

'Do you?' His voice was colder now. 'I rather gathered from your letter that I was the last person you wanted.'

'I know, and I'm sorry.' She looked at him with unshed tears sparkling on the end of her lashes and said quiveringly, 'But you see, I—I fell in love with someone.' He had become very still and she touched his hand gently. 'I'm sorry, Richard, I tried not to ... I didn't want ...' she broke off miserably.

'Who is it?' he asked at last.

'It doesn't matter who it was, because it's all over. It never really got off the ground, and—and I'd like to leave here now as quickly as possible. If you'll help me, please.'

'You'd better tell me what's happened,' Richard said grimly.

'Yes, I will, later. But first I want you to make out a deed of gift. You can do that in Austria, can't you?' Lee asked anxiously.

'Why, yes, but ...'

'Please, Richard, don't ask any questions now. Look, there's paper and a pen here.'

He was about to argue, but after a long look at her stricken face, said reluctantly, 'All right, what are the details?'

He seated himself at a massive desk ornamented with brass inlay, and Lee replied, 'I want to make an unconditional gift, to take effect immediately, of the Chalet Alpenrose and the land that goes with it, to Herr von Reistoven.'

Richard opened his mouth to protest, then shut it again grimly and began to write. Lee took another piece of paper and wrote a short, very terse note. 'I know about the toll-road and the hotel you intend to build on the Alpenrose estate. You must have wanted it very badly to even be willing to marry me. I make you a gift of it. I want neither the Chalet Alpenrose nor you so badly that I would be willing to live a lie.' With shaking hands she put down her pen and folded the paper.

'You'll have to sign this,' Richard told her. 'And I'll witness your signature.' But when she went to sign it he stopped her and said, 'Lee, do you realise what you're giving up?'

She turned to look at him, her eyes haunted, her face ashen. 'Yes, I know exactly what I'm giving up.' Richard witnessed her signature and Lee put the deed and her note in an envelope and wrote Max's name on it. She would have to write to Anna von Reistoven later and apologise for not saying goodbye.

'Richard, do you have a car here?' she asked.

'Yes, I hired one at the airport. I left it in the road outside the castle. I'll go and bring it in and you can ...'

'No, don't bring it into the Schloss. The road continues alongside the wall to another gate further on. Will you drive the car round to there and wait for me? I have to pack.'

'Why don't you just ring for the maid, or butler, and tell them to bring the cases to that courtyard I came through?' Richard asked.

'Because I don't want anyone to know I'm leaving.'

'Lee, what's been happening here? Why all the secrecy?'

'I can't explain now, there isn't time. Please trust me, Richard, I'll tell you everything when we get home.'

He looked at her searchingly. 'All right, if that's the

way you want it. I'll go and get the car.'

Quickly Lee ran back to her room and propped the letter for Max on the dressing table. It didn't take long to throw her belongings into her suitcases; taking them down the back stairs without being seen was more difficult, but luckily the servants were all in the kitchens preparing dinner, so she was able to reach Richard undetected.

'Is that the lot?' he asked, putting the cases in the boot.

'Yes. Please, Richard, let's go quickly.'

He glanced at her face, then grimly started the engine and sent them speeding from the castle.

CHAPTER TEN

FILLED with an overpowering sense of desolation, Lee sat silently in the car as they drove through the village and out towards the other side of the valley. She was trying not to think, not to feel. Gradually they began to climb up the switchback mountain road that would lead them to a pass through the Alps, and then, Lee knew, the valley would be gone for ever. On impulse she put out a hand to touch Richard's arm.

'There's a place just ahead where you can park and look back down the valley. Could we stop there for a few minutes, please?'

'Are you sure that's wise, Lee? You'll only be turning the knife in the wound,' he told her, anxiety for her in his eyes.

'Just for a minute, that's all.'

He nodded reluctantly and drove right to the front of the observation platform. A coach-load of tourists, taking photographs or looking through binoculars, obscured the view, so Lee got out to find a space where she could see. The air was cooler up here and made the green valley with its little towns nestling in the sun seem a world away. Lee felt as if she was leaving a place of warmth and laughter to enter one of grey bleakness as cold as the mountain peaks around her. Only the road joined the two worlds as it wound like a long serpent for miles back down the valley. Cars crawled slowly round the hairpin bends, hugging the mountainside away from the sheer drop below, but far away, almost on the valley floor, Lee could see a car driven at speed, honking furiously until a coach pulled over and it flashed past seemingly within a few inches of the edge. The driver must be a maniac, Lee thought as the tyres of the big grey car screeched round a bend taken much too fast. A big grey car! She grabbed the binoculars from the hands of a startled tourist standing next to her and trained them on the speeding vehicle. It was Max! She would know that car anywhere.

With a yelp she pushed the glasses back into the man's hands and sprinted for the car. 'Richard, get going, quickly! He's coming after us!'

'What! You mean ...'

'Yes. Please hurry.'

'I'm not running away from ...'

'But I am! Richard, if you don't drive this thing, I'll drive it myself. Move over!'

'On this road?' He started the engine and pulled back on to the road. 'But I hate running like this.'

'Oh, never mind that, just drive. Can't you go any faster?' She peered anxiously through the back window.

Richard shot her a look, but obligingly overtook two cars before quickly pulling back in to avoid one coming the other way. As they reached the pass he was able to go even faster and Lee's hopes began to rise, but then they got held up behind a slow-moving caravan that was just beginning the descent of the other side. Far back at the beginning of the pass Lee saw a grey car nose past another coach and begin to thunder towards them.

'Richard, hurry! He's gaining on us.'

A small gap in the oncoming traffic appeared and Richard was through. In a trice they were rushing down the switchback at a speed that took Lee's breath away and left them only a margin of safety. But Max hadn't left himself even that; he came screeching round the bends with burning tyres and all the skill of a racing driver.

'We don't stand a chance against that car,' Richard said after a glance in the mirror. 'There's a side road to the left down in the next valley. If I can get far enough ahead of him the bend will hide us while I pull into it.'

He put his foot down as they reached the valley floor and they drew ahead while Max still tore down the hairpins, then Richard stood on the brakes and swung the wheel to the left as they bolted into a road shrouded by trees. Frantically Lee looked through the rear window. Would their ruse work? There was no sign of the Mercedes and she turned and pummelled Richard exultantly on the shoulder.

'We've done it! We've lost him!'

'Afraid not, Lee,' Richard said ruefully, his eyes on the rear mirror. 'Here he comes.'

The grey car was only a few hundred yards behind them when Max put his hand on the horn and held it there. The powerful motor seemed to surge towards them.

'Damn him, I'm not pulling up,' Richard said between his teeth, but then the Mercedes was alongside and was moving over towards them, crowding them off the road. 'He's trying to force us off the road! Why, the crazy ...' His words were lost as he hit a small rock on the verge and went careering down a bank to come to a halt in a grassy meadow.

For several seconds Lee sat there, too stunned to move, then, with trembling fingers, she unfastened her safety belt. After one glance to make sure she wasn't hurt, Richard was out of the car, but Max had already left the Mercedes on the road and raced round to Lee. Throwing open the door, he took hold of her arm and roughly pulled her out.

'I want to talk to you,' he said grimly.

Suddenly Lee was gloriously angry. 'Are you crazy? You could have killed us, do you know that?' she yelled at him.

Richard ran up beside her and added his voice to hers. 'You maniac! I'm going to call the police and have you arrested! What the hell did you do a thing like that for?'

Max opened his mouth to say something, but couldn't make himself heard.

'I hope you do get arrested. I hope you go to jail for years and years!'

'Don't you know you scared the life out of Lee? You shouldn't be allowed on the roads!'

Exasperated beyond patience, Max gave Richard a push that sent him flat on his back, said, 'Will you shut up?' and taking hold of Lee tried to carry her towards his car.

With a howl of rage Richard leapt to his feet and tore a struggling Lee from Max's arms. 'Take your hands off my girl!' he yelled.

Lee found herself sprawling on the ground as Max

unceremoniously dropped her to defend himself. Dazedly she stared up as the two men wrestled together, each trying to knock the other down. Before she recollected that she ought to be stopping the fight, it was all over. Richard took Max by surprise and hit him with a punishing right hand that caught him off balance and sent him crashing to the ground.

'Max!' Lee gave a cry of fright and ran to fling herself on her knees beside his prone body.

'Come on, Lee. Leave him! Let's get out of here.'

'But he's hurt. He might have fractured his skull!'

'No, he's only stunned. Come on, you drive my car back on to the road while I take the rotor-arm out of his engine. We can be across the border before he gets it fixed.'

'But, Richard, I can't leave him like this.'

'I tell you he'll be all right,' Richard said impatiently, and was about to add a good deal more, but just then Max groaned and sat up, a hand to his jaw.

'Max, are you all right?' Lee asked anxiously.

'He knocked me down!' he said in amazement. He was so big that it had obviously never happened to him before, and he seemed more stunned by this than by the blow. His hands balled into fists and a vengeful gleam came into his eyes, so Lee said hastily.

'I'm not surprised. He was the boxing champion of his university for two years, and he's a judo black belt,' she added for good measure.

'He is?' A wary look came into Max's eyes as he got to his feet and pulled her up beside him. Richard had gone away in disgust and was examining his car.

Seeing this, Max pulled Lee towards some trees at the edge of a wood and hurried her along regardless of her efforts to get free until they came to a grassy clearing where rays of sunlight shafted down through the branches.

'Why did you run away?' he asked abruptly.

'You read my note. I should think that explains everything,' she said coldly.

'*Mein Gott*, you really believed that of me!' Max spoke half to himself, disbelief in his voice. Suddenly he caught hold of her by the shoulders, his eyes dark with rage and hurt, almost shaking her in his anger. 'Are you never going to learn to trust me?' he said harshly. 'You'd rather believe the gossip of a serving-maid than me, wouldn't you? Ever since I've known you you've been ready to believe the worst of me. Even now—after we ...' he broke off, his breathing unsteady. With a tremendous effort he controlled his emotion and when next he spoke his voice was heavy with sarcasm. 'Well, for your information, the road and the hotel are being built in a completely different valley, in an entirely different region of the Tyrol. You could have found that out quite easily for yourself if you'd bothered to come and ask me. I'd even have shown you the plans, just like I offered to show you the proof of the chalet's ownership. But you couldn't do that, could you?' he went on inexorably. 'You naturally credited me with every dishonourable purpose you could think of, and then made your noble little gesture before sneaking out of the back door!'

Lee stared at him, her face ashen. 'Max, I ...'

'Well, here's your precious chalet back, Lee.' He took the deed of gift from his pocket and savagely tore it into shreds. 'Do what you like with it. I never really cared whether you sold it to me or not. From the moment I met you all I wanted was you!' He turned on his heel and strode a few yards away to stand against a tree trunk, his back towards her.

Lee gazed after him, unable to speak, unable to find any words to ask him to forgive her. All she could do was to imploringly say his name. 'Max!'

It seemed an age before he turned to face her, his features set in grim lines. Then slowly his expression changed. 'Come here,' he said sternly.

On shaking legs she slowly went to stand a few feet away from him, her eyes never leaving his face. 'You crazy little fool!' Max opened his arms and she gave a choking cry of thankfulness as she ran into them. She tried to talk to him, to tell him how sorry she was, but he wouldn't let her. He kept calling her a lovely little fool, a beautiful idiot, telling her she deserved a good spanking, so in the end she gave up and stopped him with her lips. He took them savagely and his kisses became possessively demanding.

'*Liebchen*, I want you so much,' he said huskily. 'Did you really think that I would ever let you go? When they told me that you had driven off with another man ... *Gott*, it was pure hell until I read your note and realised why you'd gone. Oh, Lee, marry me soon.'

'Just as soon as you want.' Breathlessly she returned his kiss. 'People will think I'm marrying you for your money,' she said, half teasing, half serious.

He laughed. 'After all the trouble I've had in getting you to admit you love me!' He began to undo the top button of her blouse and his voice became muffled as he kissed her shoulder, the curve of her breast.

'Hey,' Lee said softly. 'Have you forgotten Richard?'

Reluctantly Max straightened up. 'I suppose we shall have to go and find him. He's probably told the police that I've kidnapped you by now.' He put a fingertip where his lips had touched her breast. 'Remember where I got to. I may need to find that place again.'

Lee looked mistily up at him. 'I'll bear it in mind.'

But when they emerged hand-in-hand from the wood only the Mercedes was to be seen.

'He's gone!' Lee exclaimed. 'And he's put my cases in your car.'

'He's left us a note,' Max said as he saw a piece of paper propped up against the steering wheel. 'It says, "Old Chinese proverb: He who wins fight loses girl." You know, I think I might have liked your unofficial fiancé, even after all the things I've been wishing him these last weeks. He's a good loser. Perhaps we could invite him to the wedding, and we'll have all your family and friends fly out for it too.'

Lee reached out to gently stroke his cheek. 'Thank you, I'd like that.'

Her fingers wandered to the silky hairs that curled at the back of his neck. Max drew in his breath sharply and bent to kiss her compulsively.

'Where shall we go for our honeymoon?' Lee asked at last, her arms around his neck.

'There's a certain mountain hut I know of,' Max ventured.

'But I haven't a thing to wear that's suitable for mountain huts,' Lee pretended to pout.

'How about that dress you wanted to wear to the Opera Ball?' Max suggested mockingly.

'But that wouldn't be suitable for a mountain hut!' she objected.

'On the contrary, my love, I think it very suitable.'

At the sight of Lee's blushing cheeks, Max chuckled and drove them decorously home to the Schloss Reistoven.

Harlequin

COLLECTION

EDITIONS OF 1978

Harlequin's Collection

ANDREA BLAKE
**Night of
the Hurricane**

Harlequin's Collection 105   1.25

ANNE WEALE
**If This
Is Love**

**50 great stories
of special beauty
and significance**

$1.25
each novel

In 1976 we introduced the first 100 Harlequin Collections—a selection of titles chosen from our best sellers of the past 20 years. This series, a trip down memory lane, proved how great romantic fiction can be timeless and appealing from generation to generation. The theme of love and romance is eternal, and, when placed in the hands of talented, creative, authors whose true gift lies in their ability to write from the heart, the stories reach a special level of brilliance that the passage of time cannot dim. Like a treasured heirloom, an antique of superb craftsmanship, a beautiful gift from someone loved—these stories too, have a special significance that transcends the ordinary. **$1.25 each novel**

Here are your 1978
Harlequin Collection Editions...

Original Harlequin Romance numbers in brackets

ORDER FORM
Harlequin Reader Service

In U.S.A.
MPO Box 707
Niagara Falls, N.Y. 14302

In Canada
649 Ontario St.,
Stratford, Ontario, N5A 6W2

Please send me the following Harlequin Collection novels. I am enclosing my check or money order for $1.25 for each novel ordered, plus 25¢ to cover postage and handling.

□ 102	□ 115	□ 128	□ 140
□ 103	□ 116	□ 129	□ 141
□ 104	□ 117	□ 130	□ 142
□ 105	□ 118	□ 131	□ 143
□ 106	□ 119	□ 132	□ 144
□ 107	□ 120	□ 133	□ 145
□ 108	□ 121	□ 134	□ 146
□ 109	□ 122	□ 135	□ 147
□ 110	□ 123	□ 136	□ 148
□ 111	□ 124	□ 137	□ 149
□ 112	□ 125	□ 138	□ 150
□ 113	□ 126	□ 139	□ 151
□ 114	□ 127		

Number of novels checked @
$1.25 each = $ _____
N.Y. and N.J. residents add
appropriate sales tax $ _____

Postage and handling $ ____.25

                                    TOTAL $ _____

NAME _____
                    (Please Print)
ADDRESS _____

CITY _____

STATE/PROV. _____

ZIP/POSTAL CODE _____

ROM 2185

Offer expires December 31, 1978